"You are obviously an educated man," Tom said. "Your speech indicates that. What I don't understand is why someone with so superior an intellect and great leadership potential for his people, would take them down such a disastrous and stupid path to destruction."

"*I* do nothing, Cuchillo Largo," the Indian said. "It is Thunder Eagle who speaks through me and I am merely an implement of his bidding."

Brujo, the medicine man, could stand no more of this talk. "Liar! Crazy man! The great god Thunder Eagle spits on you. You are—"

The nearest guard's lance struck out, stabbing the old man in the side, and immediately Tom's *katana* flew from its scabbard and sent the attacker's head to the ground. The second guard made a quick move toward Tom, then immediately stumbled back with both hands gone, but still clutching the lance where they lay in the dirt. Tom raised his sword and cut the hapless man from shoulder to waist in a quick but easy slice. The body tumbled to El Mesias's feet. The Indian, unshaken, looked down on the hunks of meat that once made up his two bodyguards.

"Your skill with the sword has been related to me many times," he said. "Now I know all those stories were true."

"Would you test my blade?"

"Perhaps. But not now. Thunder Eagle may decide to with his lightning, and that will be the end of Cuchillo Largo," El Mesias said. "It is true you can defeat most men with your speed and sharp blade, but you are not an Indian—no matter what ceremonies you have participated in—and that will be your death warrant as it is to all White-Eyes in this land."

The Six-Gun Warrior Series:

#1 SIX-GUN SAMURAI
#2 BUSHIDO VENGEANCE
#3 GUNDOWN AT GOLDEN GATE
#4 KAMIKAZI JUSTICE
#5 THE DEVIL'S BOWMAN
#6 BUSHIDO LAWMAN
#7 PRAIRIE CAESAR

SIX-GUN WARRIOR

APACHE MESSIAH

by Patrick Lee

PINNACLE BOOKS **NEW YORK**

SIX-GUN WARRIOR #8: APACHE MESSIAH

Copyright © 1983 by Patrick E. Andrews

An original Pinnacle Books edition, published for the
first time anywhere.

First printing, May 1983

ISBN: 0-523-41499-4

Cover illustration by Bruce Minney

Printed in the United States of America

PINNACLE BOOKS, INC.
1430 Broadway
New York, New York 10018

DEDICATION

**This one is for the pickets
striking Central Graphics**

*Special thanks to Julie Stensland for
manuscript preparation.*

Prologue

In the year 1854, Commodore Perry sailed to the little known land of Japan to open commerce with that nation's reluctant authorities. After establishing a legation in Edo (a city to become known to the modern world as Tokyo), the commodore returned to the United States to file a report on the progress of his mission with the American government.

One member of that legation was young Midshipman Tommy Fletcher, a twelve-year-old bundle of boyish energy from a plantation near Wentworth, Georgia, who had been chosen to stay behind. It was thought such experience in the diplomatic world would make him a more rounded and experienced officer when he was finally qualified to receive his commission as a subaltern in the navy.

But this legation's fate was not to be a happy one. Certain elements in the Japanese hierarchy wanted the foreign devils driven from their country and kept out forever. These fanatic desires evolved into an attack on the Americans by the dreaded *ninja*—highly trained and motivated experts in espionage, assassination and sneak assaults—that left all the foreigners slaughtered, except for one: Midshipman Tommy Fletcher.

Tommy, clad only in the cut-off Japanese trousers he had learned to prefer to the more cumbersome Western style, fled into the dark night seeking safety. He melted into the population easily since his features betrayed the Cherokee blood that flowed through his veins. His black hair and dark, almond-shaped eyes caused most Japanese to mistake him for one of the hairy Ainu: the people who lived in the northernmost of Japan's island chain. The young American made ends meet by doing odd jobs in fierce competition with Japanese boys his own age. During this troubled time he not only increased his skills in hand-

1

to-hand fighting as he defended himself from attacks by contemptuous street urchins, but his naturally gifted intellect and talent enabled him to quickly pick up the complicated language of Japan until he could speak it with hardly a trace of accent.

During one of the street brawls—he had been trying to protect a few balls of rice he had earned against a gang of youths—his spirited defense and aggressive counterattacking was witnessed by a samurai named Tanaka Nobunara who was in the service of the *Shogun* Tokugawa Sama. This warrior was so impressed by Tommy's physical courage that he approached him after the fight had finally ended in the American boy's favor.

Curious about the "Ainu's" fighting ability, Tanaka Nobunara wanted to learn more about the youth. His surprise at finding out the boy was not only an American but a survivor of the attack on the legation faded in comparison to the affection that he felt for this extremely brave youngster. He invited Tommy to live in his home with him and his wife Joshi.

Joshi, like her husband, was immediately fond of the boy, and close ties among the three were quickly established. After several months it was obvious the Americans would not be returning for a long time, and the samurai and his wife formed a happy plan. They asked Tommy to become their adopted son, thus making their childless marriage a fruitful one. They promised the boy he would become a full fledged member of the samurai warrior class with all the rights and privileges as well as the awesome responsibilities and obligations. Tommy happily agreed and the necessary steps were taken. Thus Thomas Fletcher of Wentworth, Georgia, became Tanaka Ichimara Tomi and was immersed into the life of the samurai.

Twenty years passed and Tanaka Tom lost all contact with his former country. He fully accepted the philosophies, religion and spiritual beliefs of the Japanese knights he now belonged with. He was a samurai warrior serving in the Fujika *Rentai*, an elite unit of the *shogun*, when he finally received word of his American family back in Georgia.

The news was not pleasant.

There had been a great civil war in America, in which the Northern states and Southern states had fought one another in battles that would go down in the annals of mankind as the bloodiest and most brutal in history. Tanaka Tom's family had been on the Southern side—the Lost Cause—but the fate they suffered was worse than what most of the defeated endured. His two older brothers had died in the service of their state, but the most horrible fate was suffered by those members of his family who had stayed home. Yankee marauders had shown up at their plantation to do more than burn and loot. After murdering Tanaka Tom's father, they had tortured, sexually abused, and mutilated Tom's mother, sister and eleven-year-old brother. The crimes were unspeakable and brutal, more than Tanaka Tom's proud samurai soul could bear.

The news had been sent to him by a friend of the family named Tomlinson. Although the Tomlinson family's plantation was next to that of the Fletcher's, Matthew Tomlinson had been an officer in the army before the war. He did not resign his commission as did other Southerners. He stayed true to the Union and served his nation rather than his state during the terrible war years. His subsequent posting to the War Department gave him access to rosters of all the Northern units. After painstaking research he found out the unit responsible for the atrocities in Georgia. It was the 251st Ohio Volunteer Infantry Regiment, and the good general was able to acquire a roster of all who had served, beginning with their notorious commander Colonel Edward Hollister. He did not hesitate to send this information to Tanaka Tom Fletcher along with the promise of keeping him posted as to the up-to-date whereabouts of former members of that regiment of blackgaurds.

The code of the samurai—*Bushido*—demanded exact and uncompromising retribution for these wrongs. Tanaka Tom Fletcher had no choice but to leave Japan for America and, with General Tomlinson's help, track down and kill each and every member of the 251st Ohio. In the event of failure, *bushido* was extremely harsh. Tanaka Tom would be expected to take his own life through *seppuku*—ritual suicide by disembowelment.

By the time Tanaka Tom had been a year on this quest of vengeance, he had confronted and killed several members of Hollister's command in adventures that ranged from Mexico and Apache country in Arizona up to San Francisco and over to New Mexico. His final effort had ended up in his being sidetracked to the exotic locale of Nova Roma in Nebraska, where a deranged madman thinking himself a Roman emperor had forced the samurai into the dangerous life of a nineteenth century gladiator. Now, hurt and exhausted, Tanaka Tom knew he needed a rest and time to recoup both his physical and mental strength. He decided to return to the land of his friends, the Valbajo and Montalta Apaches in the Ancha Mesa of Arizona. There, with his woman Paloma, he could expect the peace and contentment of a true sanctuary.

*   *   *

Fate is inexplicable. And the interweaving of different individual destinies is complicated and unfathomable. Thus, a former boy midshipman who became a samurai warrior would one day meet an Apache savage who would become an educated man in a conflict so horrendous in scope that whole clans of a proud race would face extinction—or everlasting glory.

Strong Oak Indian Academy in Norbert, Indiana, was considered one of the leading seats of learning for American aborigines in the 1870s. Run by former Christian missionaries, this school offered the intelligent and educable young Indians a real chance at building up the intellectual muscle necessary to stand tall in the white man's complicated world.

The valedictorian of the class of 1874 was a twenty-year-old Valbajo Apache named Solomon Sonador. The graduating class, formally dressed in caps and gowns, sat in anticipation as they eagerly waited for the stunning speech this gifted young genius was sure to make. The rest of the audience, all white supporters or faculty members,

4

were also eager to hear the youthful but inspiring wisdom of this striking intellectual giant.

He walked up to the podium and stood looking out over the crowd for several long moments. Then he inexplicably raised his arms to shoulder height in a crucifixlike posture and continued looking at the people as his eyes assumed a glare that slowly grew in hate-filled intensity. Finally he stepped back from the podium and walked slowly but majestically from one end of the stage to the other before returning to where he had started. When he spoke his voice was deep and vibrating as it carried out over the stunned crowd.

"I am a Hawk of Lightning, young brother of Thunder Eagle who is the war leader of my clan and my clan's kin in the Apache nation. My brother and I, along with Spirit Woman, will make war on all white-eyes and drive them from this land of ours back across the sea to their own place of clouds and darkness. Our mission is holy, our cause just, and those that oppose us shall die as slowly as the sun crossing the summer sky. Thus I have told you what is to happen. Heed this warning and go, for from this moment on I am called El Mesias—the Messiah!"

Chapter One

The guard that manned the lookout point was only a twelve-year-old Apache boy of the Ancha Mesa clans, but he was already a combat veteran. A little more than a year ago, white renegades had attacked his village during a time when most of the warriors were away. He had stood his ground as bravely as any Apache would, and he had continued to fight until a carbine barrel had crashed down on his small skull causing a deep wound that left a jagged scar by his right eye. Too small and insignificant to be bothered with, the outlaws had left him for dead when they hauled the young girls and women back to their camp for the depraved enjoyment and pleasure the victims would provide. The boy had recovered sufficiently by the time the warriors returned to the village to be able to give them complete details of the attack. Within hours the evil men who had perpetrated the outrage were screaming their agony over Apache fires as they slowly died under torture.

A movement down the trail caught his eye, and the boy barely breathed as he waited for another glimpse of the person approaching the Ancha Mesa Apache camp. The rider came into full view within five minutes. The sight of the man brought an impromptu shout of joy to the boy's lips. He recognized him as the one white man who had proved his friendship to both the Valbajo and Montalta clans to such an extent that they had adopted him into their people as a full-fledged Apache.

"Cuchillo Largo!" the boy yelled. Then he took a deep breath and shouted out the name with every ounce of gusto his lungs could muster. "Cuchillo Largo-o-o-oooo!"

Tanaka Tom Fletcher halted his horse and glanced up the trail toward the sound. He smiled despite the pains of the mending wounds that were tightly bandaged under his padded Japanese jacket. His Apache name meant Long Knife, and it had been given him by the Valbajo medicine man after his ceremonious adoption into the clans of the Ancha Mesa Apaches. This great honor had been accorded him because of the leadership he had provided these Indians during a time when evil businessmen and politicians were trying to put a complicated plan into effect that would drive them off their gold-rich land. Only the leadership of Tanaka Tom Fletcher combined with the tenacity and bravery of the Apache warriors had brought destruction and death to those who had tried to bring about their destruction.

Tanaka Tom Long Knife urged his Morgan stallion up the winding trail toward the Valbajo camp. The foliage had grown greener and denser during his ascent from the desert floor, and even the air held a promise of coolness and refreshment. But the samuari's mind was not necessarily dwelling on the natural beauty around him. His thoughts swam with memories of the beautiful Apache woman Paloma who had accepted him as her lover during his previous visit on the Ancha Mesa. When he had left her the previous year, she had proudly told him that his child was even then growing in her belly. His reverie was broken by the sudden appearance of two grinning warriors from the trees.

"*Saludos,* Chuchillo Largo!" one called out. "It is good to have you back home again."

"Thank you, Lagarto," Tom said, recognizing the young warrior as one who was so instrumental in the great battles he had fought with these primitive people. "How goes it with the Valbajos and Montaltas?"

"Our days of glory shall never die!" Lagarto happily answered. "First Thunder Eagle sent you, now he has sent us El Mesias. We have been doubly blessed!"

Tom was puzzled. "Who is El Mesias?"

"You will see," Lagarto said. "And like all true warriors you will weep with joy and scream with rage at his words. He is our deliverer."

Tom's puzzlement at the strange declaration was overshadowed by a deep feeling of foreboding.

The battle, which had begun with a long rolling thunder of rapid gunfire, had settled down into sporadic shooting as the Apaches eased forward through the sparse cover of the mesquite toward the ranch buildings. Despite the intensity of the earlier gunplay, only two of their number had pitched lifeless to the earth. A full dozen still kept in the fight as they slowly closed in on the desperate defenders who could only catch maddeningly fleet glimpses of them.

The scene of this desperate fight was an isolated ranch some seventy miles south of where Tanaka Tom's Apache friends lived in the area known as Ancha Mesa. The defenders were the ranch owner, his wife and two hired hands. The four had barricaded themselves in the main house to fight off three times their number of determined warriors who kept the pressure on with stealth and carefully aimed shots.

One Apache warrior, although standing to the rear of his companions, kept himself exposed to the view of the ranchers as he shook his special charm toward his enemies, while maintaining a monotonous, never-ending chant. The amulet was a small gourd in which small pieces of a lightning-struck tree had been placed. These bits of wood, believed touched personally by the war god Thunder Eagle, rattled in time to the incantation of the wild-eyed Apache who continued to intone the magical words that would hurry up the destruction of the people inside the ranch building.

This particular Indian was decidedly different than the others. His face, while cruel, lacked primitiveness. A close examination would show a great light of intelligence dancing in the eyes, and his hair was not so long as the others either. But there was clear evidence it was being allowed to grow in the style of these desert dwellers.

Finally he stopped his chant and raised his arms out from his sides as if in a trance. He began to intonate again in unintelligible sounds as he gyrated closer to the fighting in a series of dancelike steps. After moving forward fifty yards, there was a definite change in his voice and facial expression as if he were actually becoming another being.

Then, with closed eyes he tipped his head back and spoke in deep, resounding tones:

"I, Thunder Eagle, speak through my little brother El Mesias. Now is the time to destroy the White-Eyes here. Do not hesitate—charge forward and kill them. Fear not death, for those Apache souls that waft above this battle will return to this earth to fight as spirit warriors. Then, after our sacred war is won, they will go to live and hunt on Mount Sagrada, where our people first appeared."

His odd behavior attracted the attention of the fighters in the ranch, and within moments four different weapons were firing at him.

"Look at El Mesias!" one warrior marveled. "None of the White-Eyes can hit him."

"He is truly protected by Thunder Eagle," another yelled. "Heed his words. Let us attack now!"

The twelve warriors leaped to their feet and ran screaming toward the adobe house. One suddenly spun and dropped under the impact of a bullet. Only a second or two later another fell in his tracks. The others pressed forward as yet one more of their number staggered back from several telling hits as the frightened ranchers increased their volume of fire. The Indians finally reached the front door of the structure and began battering at it with carbine butts. Although they were now protected and out of sight of the people inside, they could not get the heavy door to give way under the onslaught.

"Build a fire and burn through," El Mesias commanded. "Prepare yourselves to leap through the flames and kill the White-Eyes with your knives and tomahawks."

It cost two more lives to gather up fuel from the mesquite in the ranch yard, but within moments the smouldering beginnings of a fire became evident to the howling glee of the blood maddened warriors.

The three men and woman inside the building were now frantically desperate. Their ammunition was all but gone despite their employing carefully aimed shots at only the best targets. Under normal circumstances this would have

10

worked well for them. The worst thing that would have happened would be the loss of unprotected livestock driven off while the defenders were kept pinned down. But these Apaches seemed insane, caring little about damaging ranch property or stealing animals. It was undeniably apparent that this war party was after blood—and would be dissatisfied with anything less.

Even before the door had burned completely through, the fanatic warriors burst through the flaming portal with satanic screams. The first two paid for their eagerness with their lives, but the remaining five gained entrance in time to see the two hired hands blow out their own brains to avoid being captured alive. The ranch owner swung his Winchester .44 carbine toward his wife and shot her straight in the face, blowing out the back of her head. Her skirts flew as the body tumbled to the packed earth floor of the building. But before her husband could turn his weapon on himself, he was overwhelmed and dragged outside.

El Mesias stood haughtily under the wooden awning that jutted out over the now burned door. He looked down at the smoke blackened face of the struggling white man. El Mesias' voice was as cold as a mountain wind. "You will take a long time to die, White-Eyes. Your screams will reach Spirit Woman and be like music to her ears."

The rancher looked up at the strange young man who gazed down on him in a wild, wide-eyed stare. The Indian's countenance was more frightening than even the horrible death the white man knew he would endure. "God in heaven!" he cried. "Who was the demon in hell who spawned you?"

* * *

Tanaka Tom swung the Morgan stallion off the trail as his pack mule dutifully followed with the same dumb acceptance it always had for its master's activities. The samurai rode through the remaining trees and came out onto the open meadow where the wickiups of both the Valbajo and Montalta Apache clans had been established. A delegation of sorts awaited him and Tanaka Tom, de-

11

spite his fatigue and pain, smiled in recognition of two very good friends.

"Greetings, Chuchillo Largo," Osote the Valbajo said.

"*Saludos*, Chuchillo Largo," Guerrero the Montalta echoed in Spanish. "We are happy to see you again."

"And I to see you," Tanaka Tom said. He grimaced slightly as he slid from his horse and approached his friends.

"You are injured, Cuchillo Largo," Osote said. "Have you been in a great battle since last we saw you?"

"In many, *amigo*," Tom said. "And the last one left me with stiff wounds." He preferred the word stiff to painful. One striking similarity between the samurai and Apache worlds was the avoidance of complaining of any physical suffering. Thus a wound was merely something that kept a limb from moving through drawing up rather than from the pain.

Guerrero smiled. "And we know you won all those battles, Cuchillo Largo. You run from nothing, *neh?*"

"I try not to," Tom said modestly. "How are things with my friends here on the Ancha Mesa?"

"Not good," Osote said. "The young warriors have gone wild and will not listen to the counsel of the old veterans like Guerrero and me."

"Does this person called El Mesias have anything to do with it?" asked Tom.

"He has *everything* to do with it," Osote said. "But where have you heard of El Mesias?"

"I saw my friend Lagarto on the trail as I rode up the mesa," Tom explained. "He spoke glowing words of El Mesias, but my heart felt dread at the mention of this man. Who is he?"

"He was once a Valbajo," Osote explained. "Even as a boy he was very different from the rest of us. He could comprehend things like great numbers, and he learned everything taught him right away—even things that are in men's minds and cannot be shown out in the open. . . ."

"Ideas and opinions," Tom interjected.

"Yes!" Guerrero said joining in. "And he learned languages fast. He was truly a marvel, and all the people

12

looked forward to the day when he might become a shaman and guide us on our spiritual road.''

"He is not doing that now?" Tom askd.

"Yes," Osote said. "But in strange and wondrous ways. Before he was grown, some Christian missionaries took him away and put him in a White-Eye school that was special for Indian people. He stayed there many years and learned all they could teach him. Then he returned here."

"He is a leader now," Tom said. "That much I have figured out from Lagarto. But what evil does he do?"

"He would lead the Ancha Mesa clans in a war against all people," Guerrero explained. "He says that Thunder Eagle speaks through him and every Apache must listen. El Mesias claims he can kill all the White-Eyes, then he will kill other Indians and Mexicans until the Apaches are the only people on earth."

"I would learn more of this strange man," Tom said. "But first I require rest, food and water."

"There are two other things you must attend to as well," Osote said. "First you must see your woman Paloma."

"Did she have the child?" Tom asked.

"That is something you must speak to her about," Guerrero said seriously.

"Then what is the second thing I must do?" Tom asked.

"You must get your secret name from the shaman," Osote said. "All Apaches of the Ancha Mesa clans have two names. One that everyone else knows and a very special one known only to the warrior, the shaman and the gods."

"The shaman will tell me my secret name soon?" Tom asked.

"There is a ceremony," Osote said. "We will explain later. But first go to your woman. She awaits you in your old wickiup."

"Then we shall talk later," Tom said. He pulled at the reins of his animals and led them through the camp to the familiar location where he and the beautiful Paloma had established their lodge. The people greeted him solemnly

13

and with respect as was due a great warrior of their clan. And Tanaka Tom Fletcher was considered as much an Apache as any of the villagers there. He had been through the ceremony of adoption during which time he had danced himself into a trance and had spoken with both Spirit Woman and Thunder Eagle. It was these two gods who had whispered the name Cuchillo Largo to the shaman to let all know what the samurai's Apache name would be.

Finally Tom halted in front of his lodge as a wave of dizziness swept over him. He fought it down, then called out, Paloma . . . Paloma. I have returned.''

There was a rustling at the wickiup door, then Paloma emerged carrying a small bundle. Her savage beauty was just as intense as he remembered. The dark eyes snapped with primitive light, and her full, sensuous mouth displayed white even teeth that contrasted with her dark bronze skin and the long jet black tresses that streamed down her back. As she walked toward him he noted the swing of her hips, the full yet firm breasts, and the shapely calves displayed so provocatively above the high Apache moccasins. She stood in front of him, her lips formed into a proud smile. ''I told you that only a man-child could spring from the loins of a great warrior like you, Cuchillo Largo.'' She turned down a corner of the blanket to reveal a sleeping baby, its small face drawn up in a frown. ''Your son,'' Paloma said. ''I call him Pumito—Little Cougar—from the way he leaped in my womb during the time I carried him.''

Tom looked at the child noting his olive coloring and the sparse covering of black hair that adorned the little head. ''He is handsome,'' Tom said.

''As is his father,'' Paloma said. She looked up into Tom's eyes and gasped. ''You are not well, Cuchillo Largo.''

Tom tried to answer, but the scene suddenly spun in front of his eyes, and his knees gave way. He didn't feel it when he hit the ground.

Chapter Two

Captain Terrance MacNally waited as his second-in-command, a young second lieutenant just out of West Point, finished vomiting in the ranch yard. MacNally sighed. "You'd better get used to sights like that, Mister Martin. You'll be seeing a lot more Apache atrocities before this campaign is over."

Lieutenant Richard Martin spat, then stood up straight. "Sorry, Sir. Damned weak display on my part."

"Don't worry," MacNally said. "There's not a man-jack in this command that hasn't upchucked at least once after finding the remnants of a massacre and torture."

A sergeant stepped up and saluted. "Beggin' your pardon, Sir. But there ain't no more dead'uns to be found. These four was all they was."

"Thank you, Sergeant. Form a burial detail," MacNally said.

Martin watched the NCO move off to take care of the grisly task. The younger officer grimaced. "How can those savages be so . . . so damned cruel and evil?"

MacNally's mind clouded with hatred at the thought of the way Apaches made war. "If God put anything meaner than those people on this earth, we've yet to find what it is."

Martin wiped his mouth and forced himself to take another look at the burned heap of bodies beside the destroyed ranch house. "Did they torture them all to death? Even the woman?"

"I don't think so," MacNally answered. "The cadaver on the bottom shows sign of torment. I think the others were already dead when they were tossed on top of him and burned."

"They certainly didn't prepare us for anything like this at the Academy," Martin said.

"You may find this hard to believe, Mister Martin, but a year ago I was nearly court martialed for killing Apache scum—and they were from the same bunch that committed these crimes here today."

"Incredible, Sir!" Martin responded correctly.

"I was leading a patrol in pursuit of Mescalero Apaches and had tracked them into a canyon called San Felipe near the Mexican border. My scouts detected a band of Indians moving our way, and I immediately set up an ambush. When the hostiles rode into our line of fire, we opened up and pinned them down. Subsequently, we found that they weren't Mescaleros. They were Valbajos and Montaltas from the Ancha Mesa region. I immediately ordered a cease-fire, of course."

"Of course, Sir," Martin said.

"It would seem a grievous error on my part, but we subsequently found that this particular band had been doing mischief in Mexico. In fact, they had several heads of Mexican soldiers in their possession as well as rifles they were smuggling into the United States," MacNally said. "We resumed the battle but unfortunately enemy reinforcements appeared on the scene and I was forced to make a withdrawal under heavy fire."

"Most unfortunate, Sir," Martin remarked.

"Yes, Mister Martin, but the tragedy of the whole affair is that when those devils, and the white renegade who led them, was finally brought to trial, they were acquitted through some tricky, legal maneuvering by a fancy talking lawyer."

"Incredible, Sir," Martin said in sympathy.

"I received a letter of reprimand over the incident, Mister Martin, and since that time I've sworn I'll show up these Apache bastards from Ancha Mesa for exactly what they are—a band of murdering, torturing savages that must be wiped off the face of the earth."

"We certainly have the proper evidence today, Sir," Martin replied.

MacNally smiled grimly. "Indeed we do, Mister Martin. And I am about to do everything in my power to launch the United States Army into a full scale war against those devils on the Ancha Mesa!''

* * *

"Cuchillo Largo, are you awake?'' Paloma asked softly.

Tanaka Tom opened his eyes in the darkness of the wickiup. "Yes,'' he answered weakly. He felt as if his strength had been sapped, but he also experienced a strange sensation of well being and contentment. He started to sit up and Paloma helped him. "I feel strange,'' he said as she adjusted a bear robe for him to lean against.''

"The medicine man has treated your wounds with herbs and magic,'' she said. "They might have festered if he hadn't. You were sorely hurt, Cuchillo Largo.''

He nodded his head. "I know. The only thing that kept me going was the thought of Ancha Mesa . . .'' He smiled at her. ". . . and you, Paloma.''

"I am glad that picturing me in your mind gives you strength, *hombre mío*. It adds to the honor of being your woman.''

"How long have I been sleeping?'' Tom asked.

"Three days,'' Paloma answered. "You must have fought in many battles since you were last here on the Ancha Mesa. There are scars on your body I don't recall.''

"You know my body well, don't you?''

Paloma smiled. "There is not a place on your flesh I have not touched . . . or kissed.''

"When my strength returns I will take you like before,'' Tom said teasingly.

Paloma laughed. "Oh, no! You taught me many things, so I might take you first for my own pleasure, Cuchillo Largo. What do you think of that?''

"I think you are not like other Apache women.''

Once more she laughed aloud. "I am not,'' she agreed. "Your lessons of love awoke instincts in me that our people never knew lived in women's souls. That is too bad for Apache men, but very, *very* good for you!''

17

"Yes," Tom said in growing good humor. "Then in the combat of love, you are the victor and I the vanquished."

She shook her head. "No, I don't really think so, Cuchillo Largo. I will gladly surrender my body to you in any manner that suits you."

"If you continue to speak thusly, the rate of my recovery will amaze even the Valbajo's wise medicine man," Tom said.

"Then I will spend every moment speaking of our lovemaking," Paloma said leaning close to him. She brushed her lips against his gently, letting them barely touch, then she increased the pressure gradually until they both moaned in pleasure. Her tongue darted into his mouth, then she quickly broke contact and stood up. "You need rest," she said. Then she opened her buckskin robe and displayed her brown, tawny body to him. As Tom's eyes roved from her large firm breasts down to the hairy triangle between her slim, muscular thighs, he felt the stirrings of returning desire in his loins. Paloma quickly covered herself again and smiled coyly. "I did that to encourage you some," she said.

"Don't go," he said hoarsely.

"I must see to our man-child," Paloma said, going to the lodge's door. "You concentrate on getting well fast."

"I most assuredly will," Tom said sincerely.

* * *

Along the indistinct border between the United States and Mexico, there existed an underworld of cruel and desperate men who practiced outlawry against the inhabitants of both countries with cruelty and cunning. Many were well known and international reward posters were widely circulated offering top dollar for their capture or killing.

These were the less successful.

The best of this lot was an evil gang leader known as Chaparro to his men. This man carried the blood of several races in his veins. For five generations Chaparro's family had lived, fought, killed and died in the arid regions of southern Arizona and northern Mexico. His forefathers had

18

married into the area's various ethnic groups so that by the time Chaparro slipped from his mother's womb, his veins carried the blood of the Apache, the Yaqui, Mexican, and even Gringo with its several European bloodlines already established. But Chaparro inherited more than ethic qualities; he also took the natural wisdom and instinctive high intelligence his family enjoyed. Thus, while other border outlaws became known and hunted, Chaparro carried on a skillful war against the authorities and society in general without ever being positively identified. But he also played the subtle Latin American game of *mordida,* in which he paid out generous bribes to certain officials to insure his safety from official harassment. Thus he was able to operate openly and move from the shadows of the underworld to ride unmolested into any town or village without fear of arrest or other forms of reprisal.

Chaparro was a short man, standing only five and a half feet tall in his Mexican boots. Barrel chested and heavily muscled, he made up for his lack of stature with a naturally powerful physical strength and pantherlike quickness, whether wielding a knife or clearing his Colt .45 Peacemaker of leather. While most men feared him, the women he came into contact with found him irresistible. Pale blue eyes in a swarthy face wreathed by a well-kept black beard and thick heavy waves of hair had caused many a frontier lovely to lose her heart to the handsome *bandido.*

Chaparro's family boasted an unbroken line of bandit chiefs for nearly a hundred years. This monarchy, however, was not hereditary, and when Chaparro's father died his gang was suddenly rudderless with the top spot up for grabs. Chaparro naturally desired to continue the family tradition, but he knew there were several older, stronger and more experienced members of the band who also harbored ambitions to be leader. Any other upstart would have loaded his guns, sharpened his knives, then called some followers together to begin a bloodbath that would reduce the group's overall strength but at least eliminate all but one of any potential headmen.

Chaparro was above such crude tactics.

Instead he followed the simple expediency of poisoning any potential adversaries. It was easy enough to do. He simply waited for a moonless night, then went to several cookfires and dropped *veneno de hombre,* a potent Indian concoction, into the pots that customarily simmered overnight for the next day's breakfast. Although several innocent persons were also caught up in the murders and died coughing, vomiting deaths, there was no one else to challenge his bid for leadership. The other gang members accepted him and the family custom of bandit chiefship continued on unchallenged.

Chaparro's leadership was permanently established after a couple of years of actual operations. His success rate was phenomenal, and his followers enjoyed the best in loot and women as well as freedom from capture or harassment by the authorities. Such accomplishments bring about the hero worship and faith a good leader needs when directing activities taking place within violent and dangerous circumstances.

The main reason for Chaparro's success was his well-organized intelligence net. Rather than harass helpless, poverty-stricken *péones* for sport as did other bandits, Chaparro not only left them in peace, but also brought them gifts of grain, rice, beans or even money whenever possible. This, combined with the protection he afforded numerous villages, guaranteed him freedom from betrayal as well as hundreds of people who voluntarily and quite happily kept him completely informed of activities along the border.

At the time of Tanaka Tom Fletcher's return to the Valbajo Apache camp on the Ancha Mesa, Chaparro's band of a hundred *pistoleros* as well as camp followers and slaves, had been resting up after an extensive campaign of raiding the central highlands of Mexico. Chaparro was into his second *siesta* of the day when he was awakened and told that a *péon* from north of the town of Escondido, Mexico, had arrived in camp with information that might prove useful. Ever the opportunist, Chaparro bid the poor farmer be brought into his presence for an immediate audience.

20

The man, clad in the white pajama-type costume of his class, shuffled forward on sandaled feet, holding his sombrero respectfully in his hands. He bowed politely and smiled. "I am called Jorge Castillo, *Don* Chaparro," he said in way of introducing himself.

Chaparro returned the smile. "*Mucho gusto, Señor* Castillo," he said courteously. Any other less intelligent bandit would have contemptuously addressed the *péon* by his first name and even bullied him. But Chaparro knew such crude conduct did not buy the respect and affection of people who could prove useful to him. "Will you take some *café* with me, *Señor?*"

"Yes, *por favor*," Jorge Castillo said. "I have come a long *distancia, Don* Chaparro."

"Then please take a seat," Chaparro said. "Somebody bring *Señor* Castillo a chair, *pronto!*"

One was promptly produced and the *péon* sat down in time to be handed a cup of hot coffee. "You are very kind—*muy bueno—Don* Chaparro."

"*Es mi gusto*," Chaparro entoned in the traditional manner of a good host. He allowed Jorge Castillo to drink his coffee before he got to the point. "You have information for me?"

"Yes, *Don* Chaparro. It is possibly useless and I beg your forgiveness for probably wasting your time."

"I appreciate you taking the time to visit me, no matter what the value of your information, *Señor*," Chaparro said.

"You are *muy simpático, Don* Chaparro," Jorge Castillo said. He paused a few moments. "My information concerns the Apaches that live across the border at the place known as Ancha Mesa."

"The Valbajos and Montaltas?" Chaparro asked.

"Yes. Raiding parties are coming out of their camps," the *péon* said.

Chaparro was suddenly interested. "*¡Qué raro!* Those *indios* have been well behaved for quite a long time. What has made them turn to war?"

"A new leader called El Mesias," Castillo answered.

21

"My cousin Lorenzo heard all about him in Escondido where he works for the gun dealer Avila. One of El Mesias' men bought repeating rifles there and told about how one of the Apache gods speaks through this new leader. They think they can destroy all the *gringos*, and afterwards the *mexicanos* too."

"Are they going to raid in Mexico?" Chaparro asked.

"They already have, *Don* Chaparro," Castillo answered. "And since the Mexican government will pay for Apache scalps, I thought you would be interested."

"*Por su puesto*, I certainly am," Chaparro said. "And if they are playing the devil up in the *Estados Unidos*, the American army will not object if I wage war against the Ancha Mesa Apaches."

"I think not, *Don* Chaparro," Castillo said. "I would believe the American authorities would look upon scalp hunting expeditions as a blessing—forgive my boldness at giving my opinion."

"Your opinion is appreciated, as is your kindness for bringing me this information, *Señor* Castillo," Chaparro said. He motioned to one of his lieutenants standing nearby. "Raul, fetch ten pesos for our good friend here. And see that he is well fed and provisioned before he leaves us to return to his village."

Jorge Castillo smiled in genuine appreciation. "You are most kind—*como siempre*—like always, *Don* Chaparro."

Chaparro, now all business, waved the *péon* away as he turned to his most trusted subordinates seated around him. "Do any of you know the price on scalps now?"

"I do, *jefe mío*," one said with a wide grin. "Twenty-five pesos for each adult male, fifteen pesos for a woman, and five for a child no matter the sex."

Chaparro laughed aloud baring his tobacco-stained teeth. "Then even the babies on the Ancha Mesa will add to our growing wealth, *muchachos*." He stood up. "I am taking three men with me to Escondido to recruit some more *hombres* to ride with us. When I return I will expect all of you to be prepared to go as far north as the *gringo* border if necessary to slaughter the Valbajos and Montaltas.''

Several cheers sounded spontaneously. "We will be ready, *Jefe*," one bandit shouted. "With guns loaded and scalping knives sharpened—and pursestrings loosened for the pesos to be earned from Apache lives!''

Chapter Three

Dawn had just begun its red glowing ascent of the eastern hills when Tanaka Tom's eyes opened. He breathed deeply for several long moments as he tested his alertness and general condition. His wounds were not too stiff, and he noted with satisfaction that most of the irritating pain had now subsided to a dull ache that he could easily ignore.

Paloma still slept at his side, her breathing soft and deep. Tom slid his hand over and ran it along her naked side down to the firm muscle of her upper leg. Then he gently eased his probing fingers to the softness of her inner thigh and gently stroked her. She stirred slightly and slowly opened her eyes looking into his face. *"Buenos días,"* she greeted him with a lazy smile.

"Good morning to you," Tom said slipping closer to her warm body. His fingers now found the moist opening at the bottom of her torso, and he gently probed there until he found the place he was searching for.

"Oooh, Cuchillo Largo," she sighed softly. "You are healthy again, no?''

Tom kissed her full lips. "Find out for yourself, *mujer mía.*''

"I like it when you call me your woman—*tu mujer*— because that's what I am," Paloma said. Her own hand explored his body and slipped down to his member. "Ay! It stands like sturdy pine on the mountain top. What do you require then, *hombre mío?*''

23

"You don't know?" Tom asked.

"I want *you* to tell *me*," Paloma said teasingly. "You have not taken all the Apache instincts out of me. I still want my man to tell me what he wants—and I will see that he is satisfied."

"I want you to go down to it," Tom said.

"Yes, *amor mío*," Paloma responded. She kissed his mouth then let her lips travel from his face to his chest. After several long caresses on his belly with her tongue, she continued until his erect manhood was next to her mouth. Within moments she gently applied herself in movements that gradually increased in speed until the Sixgun Samurai groaned in pleasure. Finally he eased her away from him. "Enough."

"No!" she protested in a frantic whisper. "You have not expelled your love juice."

"Remember what I taught you of peaks and valleys?" he asked. "We mustn't make love in frantic haste like forest animals. Sexual union between man and woman is a gentle thing that must be drawn out and sustained with delightful teasing and brief moments of respite."

"And I have learned that lesson well, *hombre mío*," Paloma said. "As you will quickly find out." She went back to her task and worked him up until she sensed the sensitive moment was near, then she gradually slowed down to a stop before once again repeating the procedure. Finally she sensed the time was right and brought him to the moment of fulfillment. As he recovered, she brought her face back up to his. "Could any Japanese woman do it as well?"

"I don't think so," Tom whispered sincerely.

"Ha!" Paloma said with satisfaction. "They are not savage enough for you. Only an Apache woman can bring you complete satisfaction—and of all the women of my clan, I am the best for you, *que no?*"

"Que, sí," Tom agreed. He kissed her gently, then slipped his tongue between her lips as she began her own frantic moaning. He cupped one large breast, but Paloma quickly pushed his hand away.

"No!"

"What?" Tom asked puzzled.

"They are full of milk for our man-child, Cuchillo Largo. This is not the time for your caresses there," she explained. "I feel no pleasure at your touch."

Tom nodded his understanding and placed his hand between her legs on the triangle of hair there. "How is that?" he asked.

"Oh, yes, *hombre mío*, that is where I want you," Paloma whispered with her lips close to his ear. Tom started to move down, but once again she stopped him. "Cuchillo Largo, I want this, not your mouth," she said, grasping his manhood. "It has been too long since your seed has been inside me, and I desire nothing else more at this moment."

Tom rolled over as she spread her legs wide for him. "I will do as you want then, Paloma," he said.

"*Entreme, hombre mío*, and don't be gentle . . . I want you to ravish me like a warrior would a captive maiden!"

Tom responded as his savage woman groaned and writhed under his muscular body. She bit and scratched him as her primitive desires took over her soul and dominated every sensation of her being.

* * *

The sentry presented arms as Captain Terrance MacNally and Second Lieutenant Richard Martin led their patrol back into Fort Bozie, Arizona Territory. They halted in front of their troop headquarters, and the two officers dismounted as two orderlies hurried forward to take charge of their horses.

MacNally ignored proper protocol as he called out to his senior sergeant. "Dismiss the patrol after the mounts are stabled and rubbed down, Sergeant."

"Yes, Sir," the NCO said. He started to salute but his commanding officer had already turned away and was hurrying across the parade ground toward post headquarters.

MacNally and Martin walked into the building and paused before the adjutant's desk. "Is Colonel Breckenridge in?"

"Yes, Sir," the adjutant replied. "I'll announce you, Sir." The officer opened the commander's door and barely

25

had time to open his mouth before MacNally stormed past him.

"By God, we got the sons of bitches this time, Sir!" MacNally happily exclaimed.

"Ancha Mesa Apaches on the warpath for sure?" the colonel asked, looking up from the quartermaster report he had been studying.

"There's no denying it," MacNally said. "With the evidence of this last raid we might even be able to bring that damned-to-hell Thomas Fletcher back for trial too—if we can find out where he is."

"A quick verbal report on the patrol, if you please, Captain MacNally," Colonel Breckenridge said with some annoyance that the junior ranking officer had not saluted properly when he entered his office.

"Yes, Sir," MacNally said. He gave a quick run-down on the atrocities committed on the ranch where they had found the murdered woman and men. He continued on about several arrows as well as a broken lance found on the scene that were easily identifiable as belonging to the Ancha Mesa Apache clans. To substantiate the findings, MacNally's patrol had trailed the raiders back to the foothills of their territory and every soldier in the detail had been asked to personally note that the track left by the Apaches, as faint as it was, undeniably led up to their stronghold. "We'll hang those savage bastards yet for the humiliation they caused us to suffer after the trial in Lone Gap."

Colonel Breckenridge's mood brightened. "It appears that we shall," he agreed. "And if there is any way at all we can tie that Fletcher fellow into this, I want it done."

"I'm certain we can, Sir," MacNally said. "If he's anywhere in Arizona territory, that is."

"I'm placing you personally in charge of this operation, Captain MacNally," the colonel said. "You are to take command of 'K' and 'M' troops as well as your own. I want your squadron to devote twenty-four hours a day to the destruction of those Apache devils once and for all. I won't rest until every last one of them has been killed or driven off the Ancha Mesa."

26

"Yes, sir!" MacNally saluted and left the office with Lieutenant Martin following on his heels. When they were outside he paused and turned to his subordinate. "Ready for some real campaigning now, Mister Martin?"

"Of course, Sir," the youngster answered.

"Fine. Because as of right now we're at war," MacNally said grimly. "Within four hours of organizing the squadron, I want it out of this garrison, fully armed and equipped, heading straight for Ancha Mesa. We'll wipe those goddamned Apaches right off the face of God's green earth. And this time I'll personally guarantee it!"

* * *

Tanaka Tom Fletcher lounged outside the wickiup with his shirt off. The warm afternoon sun worked as a balm on his healing wounds while it relaxed and loosened the sorely tired muscles he had worked so hard during his ordeal as a gladiator under the madman in Nova Roma. The peace and tranquility he needed for his emotional recovery seemed to end almost immediately with the excited arrival of the young warrior Lagarto. Even Paloma, sitting beside her man nursing their child, sensed trouble as Lagarto strode up boastfully.

"*Saludos,* Cuchillo Largo," Lagarto said smiling widely.

"Greetings, Lagarto," Tanaka Tom answered. "Sit down with me. I'm sorry I haven't had much of a chance to speak with you since my return, but I was occupied with other things."

"And I've been busy as well, Cuchillo Largo. That is why I am here. I wish to speak with you."

Tanaka Tom nodded his assent. "I have heard from both Osote and Guerrero that there are many exciting things happening on the Ancha Mesa."

Lagarto spat and, to Tom's surprise, spoke disrespectfully of the two older warriors. "That pair makes me sick and ashamed, Cuchillo Largo. They have turned into doddering old widows, lost and without heart or courage."

Tom's jaw tightened but nothing else betrayed his annoyance with the young man. "I have fought in many

27

battles with Osote and Guerrero. Always they were in the thick of the fight, brave and fierce."

"They've changed since El Mesias arrived," Lagarto said. "This wondrous man, through whom the great war god Thunder Eagle speaks, has brought us a chance to rid our land of the White Eyes forever. His bravery frightens those two birds. I think they have softened so much that they squat to piss like women now."

"I would have you not talk of my two good friends in that manner," Tom said in a serious tone.

"I speak of cowards as I please," Lagarto said. "And you are an Apache with an Apache name. You, like all warriors of the Ancha Mesa, must make a choice."

"Must I?" Tom asked. "I feel no pressure from *anyone* to do *anything*."

Lagarto, realizing his arrogance, smiled and calmed down a little. "Of course, Cuchillo Largo. You have proven yourself a brave warrior and you don't know the full story of what great things are happening to us. I am sure when you find out, you will be as excited as I."

Tom pondered the true meaning behind Lagarto's words. "How are the Thunder Eagles?" he asked. This warrior society was one he had formed during the last troubles that afflicted both the Valbajo and Montalta clans.

"They no longer exist as you knew them," Lagarto answered. "Almost all ride with El Mesias now. They have participated in great victories."

Tanaka Tom laughed derisively. "*Great victories?* Osote tells me that El Mesias rode off Ancha Mesa with twelve good warriors and returned with only five. A few more *great victories* like that and there will be no more Valbajo or Montalta warriors to win honors."

Lagarto leaped to his feet and shouted, "See? You are as ignorant as those two fools! The ghosts of the slain warriors ride with us through El Mesias' medicine. They do mischief to our enemies while we fight them. They hide their bullets. Push their rifle barrels aside. Throw dust in their eyes. That way we have a great advantage and will drive these interlopers from our land forever."

"I have no faith in El Mesias," Tom stated flatly.

"You must talk with him," Lagarto said, trembling with rage. "Then you will know he is truly great and has been blessed by Thunder Eagle."

"Then tell him to come see me," Tom said.

"A man who is a soul mate with Thunder Eagle does not seek audience with any other," Lagarto said. "You must go to him, Cuchillo Largo."

"I do not wish to speak with him," Tom said. "But I would speak with the Thunder Eagles. They are brave warriors and I have fought alongside them against evil men who would have destroyed both clans of the Ancha Mesa."

Lagarto, despite his primitive background, recognized the diplomatic situation Tom was proposing. If either Cuchillo Largo or El Mesias happened to be visiting the Thunder Eagles and the other showed up, it would not actually be a direct visit of one upon the other. That way neither would lose face or dignity. Lagarto squatted down. "When do you wish to speak with them? I know them all, of course, and they would be happy to see the great warrior Cuchillo Largo who led them to such glorious victories last year."

"I would be pleased to visit with my old friends at any time," Tom said, opening the door even farther. "Perhaps it would be best if you told me when they might be gathered in one spot."

"*Es bueno,* Cuchillo Largo," Lagarto said. "I will find out when they might gather and return to you. Perhaps El Mesias will be there too. If so, I advise you to listen to him. To do otherwise would make you an old widow like Osote and Guerrero are." He stood up to walk away. "And you know what we Apaches do with our useless widows, don't you?"

Tom, his expression unchanged, nodded affirmatively. The unfortunate women were generally tied to trees and left to the mercy of the elements or roving predators. No matter which, the result was always the same—death.

Chapter Four

Capitán Francisco Moreno of the Mexican *Rurales* had just stretched out on the crude bunk behind the desk in his office when the excited voice of a tower sentry interrupted his plans for a quiet *siesta*.

Grumbling under his breath, he got to his feet and pulled on a soiled jacket bearing the once glittering shoulder straps that denoted his rank in the provincial police.

"*¿Qué pasa?*" he asked of the sergeant hurrying across the parade ground toward him.

"Three riders approaching, *mi capitán*," *Sargento* Romero replied. "I have put the garrison on full alert."

"*¿Qué?* For three men?" Moreno asked astounded.

"We think it might be Chaparro," Romero explained. "That means there must be anywhere from fifty to a hundred *bandidos* just over the horizon out of sight."

"You are right," Moreno said. "Keep the men at their posts until further orders." This particular station was typical of the *rurale* forts that dotted the Sonoran desert south of Arizona Territory. There were no building materials available—trees were scarcer even than water, and the sandy terrain was unsuitable for adobe—so the garrison's defenses were earthen and simple. Trenches had been dug, and the earth taken from the ground was put in wicker baskets to add both height and depth to the overall defenses. The headquarters building, jail and barracks were constructed of adobe bricks brought in from Nogales. The dominating feature of the small post was the lookout tower on top of the main structure. Being stationed as a guard in this rickety contraption was the most unpopular duty of the unit assigned there.

Francisco Moreno, in the typical immodesty of Mexican

officials, had named the site Fortaleza Moreno in honor of himself.

The three horsemen rode in closer as Moreno trained his binoculars on them. Finally he nodded to *Sargento* Romero. "*¡De veras!* It is indeed our old friend Chaparro."

Romero sighed. "I hope he is here with some offer of a business deal. I am in no mood to fight him today."

"I am never in a mood to fight that *malo* . . . today or any other," Moreno said. He motioned to the guard. "Open the gate for our visitors."

"*Sí, mi capitán*," the *rurale* replied. The gate was actually a fortified wagon that was rolled back and forth to either offer or bar entrance to the center of the entrenched camp.

Chaparro and two of his lieutenants rode into the garrison and reined up in front of Moreno and his sergeant. Chaparro slid from his saddle and walked toward the captain holding out his hand in friendship. "*Buenas tardes, Capitán. ¿Como está usted?*"

"I am fine, *gracias*," Moreno replied shaking hands. "And to what do we owe the honor of this visit, *Señor* Chaparro?"

"I am here to offer my service to *la república* in these difficult times," Chaparro said.

Moreno frowned as he took a cigar offered him by one of the bandits. "And what brings about this sudden demonstration of patriotism for Mexico?"

"Have you not heard, *Señor Capitán?* There are Apaches up north who have been raiding down here, then escaping back to America."

"I know," Moreno said. "On two occasions I have seen the results of their attacks. A small *rancho* here or tiny farm there. Hardly a major war."

"But the potential is there," Chaparro said. "And I have information that there is a good chance this situation will escalate—*pronto!*"

Moreno's interest perked up. He was well aware that the bandit's intelligence net was much more far flung and efficient than his own. The captain operated in an area where the people hated the authorities with the same intensity they loathed the outlaws. Chaparro, on the other hand, broke all the rules and treated the poor quite well; therefore, they loved him and told him all they knew.

Moreno cleared his throat. "You seem to have some definite thing to say about this Apache problem."

"I certainly do," Chaparro said. "I intend to fight the Apaches with my men whenever possible. Not only here in *la república*, but across the border as well."

"Commendable," Moreno said, feeling uneasy.

"I do not require aid from the *Rurales*," Chaparro said softly but with deadly meaning. This was his subtle way of letting Moreno know he would not tolerate him or his men in the scalp hunting expeditions he planned on conducting.

Moreno quickly took the hint, then replied in a face-saving way. "I have every confidence in your ability to effectively aid our government with this problem. However, if you ever do need help from myself or my command, please do not hesitate to ask."

Chaparro smiled and bowed. "A generous offer, *Señor Capitán*. And I appreciate it. If I do need assistance from the brave *Rurales*, I shall seek it immediately."

Moreno nodded. "*¡Bien!* Shall we have a drink together, *Señor* Chaparro?"

"I do not wish to appear ill-mannered, but the matter we are discussing is most pressing at the moment," Chaparro said, turning back to his horse. "It requires my immediate attention."

"May I ask you one question?" Moreno inquired. "Which Apache clan is involved in these raids?"

"I can tell you that," Chaparro replied generously. "They are the Ancha Mesa Apaches."

"Under Guerrero and Osote?" Moreno asked. "That does not seem like those two. I thought they were contented with the way things are for them up there."

"Those two probably are," Chaparro replied. "But there is a young hellion stirring up the warriors now. He is the war leader."

"I see," Moreno said. "Well, good luck to you and your men, *Señor* Chaparro."

"*Gracias y adiós*," Chaparro said as he wheeled his

horse and rode from the garrison with his two men following closely.

"I think I must send to Nogales for pesos to pay for Apache scalps, *Sargento* Romero," Moreno said. "The Ancha Mesa clans are going to be facing a tenacious and dangerous enemy."

Despite his hatred of Indians, Romero sadly shook his head. "May God preserve their souls. Even the children will suffer this mutilation—many while still alive."

* * *

Tanaka Tom crawled through the small opening of the wickiup, then stretched his six-foot-plus frame to its full height. He was dressed in a short kimono, held at the waist by a bright yellow *obi* (sash), and his buckskin trousers were tucked into the boot-type Apache moccasions that Paloma had made for him during his absence. He wore no head covering, and only two more items completed his wardrobe. His *katana* (long sword) and *hotachi* (short sword) were shoved into the *obi*.

Paloma joined him from the interior of their dwelling bringing Pumito with her. "Look, Cuchillo Largo! Our man-child recognizes you. See you he is smiling?"

Tom turned toward the baby and looked into the youngster's dark eyes. He grinned in spite of himself at the obvious affection being shown him. He reached out and chucked Pumito under the chin, and the baby giggled softly as if it were all a good joke.

"I am going to visit the Thunder Eagles," Tom said to Paloma.

She was surprised. "Why do you tell me where you are going, *hombre mío?* Is there some reason I must know?"

Tom shrugged. "It is a custom among my people for a man to inform his woman of such things. I am becoming more American and less Japanese with each passing day."

"You are neither now, Cuchillo Largo. You are Apache, and you must remember that."

Tom did not answer as he strode off through the village. While he admired and respected his Ancha Mesa friends, and was honored that he had been adopted into their clan,

33

he was still a samurai knight with the terrible demands of *bushido* (Code of the Warrior) burned into his soul. True he had gone into a trance and had been visited by the Apache gods Spirit Woman and Thunder Eagle, but the experience paled when compared with the spiritual teachings, demands, and philosophies of that part of Japanese culture in which he had been immersed.

Tom properly acknowledged the greetings shouted to him as he continued on his way through the unorganized maze of wickiups that made up the Ancha Mesa encampment. Even the camp dogs sensed his importance and refrained from barking at him or snapping at his heels as they generally did to casual strollers. The samurai stopped at the sight of his two good friends Osote and Guerrero. He raised his hand in greeting. ''Where are you going, old friends?''

''A little hunting,'' Osote answered. ''Perhaps such activity will take our minds off the misfortunes our people face.''

''I am going to visit the Thunder Eagles,'' Tanaka Tom Long Knife said. ''Would you go with me?''

Guerrero angrily spat. ''Never! I shall bear no more insults or stupidity from those puppies!''

''Nor I!'' Osote exclaimed.

''I must learn all I can about what is happening here,'' Tanaka Tom said. ''I will visit with you later.'' He nodded a brief goodbye, then continued on his way.

Finally the samurai reached the outer limits of the settlement and continued on up a slight grassy hill that was topped by a high stand of woods and brush. After treading along a footpath that led through the natural barrier of vegetation, he reached an opening.

A thunderous cheer broke forth from the assembly of warriors who stood there waiting for him. These fighting men were the elite of the Ancha Mesa Apaches. They formed an exclusive warrior society named the Thunder Eagles after their war god. The last time Tanaka Tom Fletcher had been on the Ancha Mesa, his Apache friends had faced complete annihilation at the hands of a crooked Indian agent named Bradford Cone. Unschooled in the tecnhiques of dirty politics and too numerically inferior to face the U.S. Army, the situation had looked bad for them until the Six-gun Samurai had taught them the military tactics he had learned during his warrior apprenticeship and active service under the *Shogun*. Tom had created a unit of shock troops to bear the brunt of the fighting and danger during the difficult time it took him to deliver his Apache friends from the insidious manipulations of Washington politicians as well as one particularly evil man named Colonel Edward Hollister.

Lagarto walked forward with a swagger, but he seemed friendly enough. "Cuchillo Largo, the Thunder Eagles greet you and welcome you back to our council fires."

Tom bowed Japanese style to the braves. "I am pleased to return, if even for a brief visit."

"Why only a short time, Cuchillo Largo," Lagarto asked. "You are an Ancha Mesa Apache, are you not?"

"I am—by your custom," Tom said.

"By *our* custom? But not *your* custom, is that not right, Cuchillo Largo?"

Tom sensed the fading friendliness as well as the growing threat in Lagarto's attitude. Here, indeed, was evidence of a friendship gone bad. But he kept his composure. "I accept my responsibilities when I am among you," he said diplomatically. "But you all know that I have a mission to accomplish that is even more important to me than my own life."

"You are either an Apache, or you are not," Lagarto said. "And you must—"

"Wait!" A voice from the rear of the throng broke over the clearing. There was some milling about as the speaker forced his way through the crowd. He was an old man, bow-legged and bent, his face and body showing the strain of his hard years as an Apache. This was Brujo, the shaman, and when he reached Tanaka Tom Long Knife and Lagarto, he shook his sacred rattle in anger at the young Apache warrior. "Shut up, young fool! You speak of matters too deep and meaningful for your empty head."

"Another of the old fools!" Lagarto yelled at the other warriors. "This doddering ancient dares to give us spiri-

35

tual advice when Thunder Eagle himself speaks to us through El Mesias!"

"Do not blaspheme the name of our great war god, you whelp!" Brujo said loudly. He turned to the throng of braves. "Listen to men who have led you to great victories. There is Osote of the Valbajos, Guerrero of the Montaltas and now Spirit Woman has guided the great Cuchillo Largo back to us in these troubled times."

The fighting men could not deny the logic or truth of the old medicine man's words. They cheered the names of the men who had brought them from the brink of destruction to complete independence from the white man and his cumbersome government regulations and interference.

"Give us your counsel, Cuchillo Largo," someone shouted. "What would you have us do?"

Tom raised his arms to quieten down the loud responses to the question. "Yes," he said. "I will advise you. And this advice for my Ancha Mesa Apache brothers comes from my heart. I want what is best for you. I have proven that. So have Osote and Guerrero. Our dedication to saving the Ancha Mesa was such that we faced death on the gallows in order to bring it about."

"What path do we follow, Cuchillo Largo?" an impatient brave asked.

"Turn from this war," Tom said bluntly. "These raids net you nothing but grief. Already you have lost too many warriors to justify the amount of booty or pale glory you can claim. The white man will become angry and strike back. What you are doing is exactly what the evil man Cone tried to get you to do. Soon soldiers will come and seek out the men guilty of these crimes. If you do not give them up, there will be a great war and many Ancha Mesa Apaches will be killed. And the others will suffer the worst death possible for proud warriors—they will become reservation Indians."

Arguments and shouting broke out among the assembled braves as they debated Tom Fletcher's words. Then suddenly they were quiet, their eyes looked up toward the highest point of the knoll they occupied. Tom turned to follow their gaze and breathed in deeply despite himself.

A magnificent figure stood there, his head adorned with a large ceremonial hat made in the shape of an eagle. The beak projected far out over the face. He wore a spotless buckskin shirt with dozens of large eagle feathers along the sleeves that gave such an elated impression that it seemed he could fly. His breech cloth, like his high-topped moccasins, was decorated with Thunder Eagle designs and other sacred symbols of the Ancha Mesa Apaches. Two warriors appeared from the woods and took protective positions on each side of the strange figure. They were similarly attired, but wore no eagle caps. Instead they wore gold-colored headbands, and their faces were painted for war.

"El Mesias!" Lagarto shouted up to him. "Come down and destroy the whimpering women who try to pass as warriors. They are an insult to true Apache blood!"

El Mesais spread his arms wide and slowly descended the gentle slope as he approached Tanaka Tom Fletcher. The samurai took a quick glance at the other warriors and noted they stood in silent awe at the imposing figure who slowly drew closer.

Finally he reached Tom and stood for several long moments staring into his face. Then he lowered his arms. "I am called El Mesias. And you are Cuchillo Largo, are you not?"

"Yes," Tom acknowledged.

"My followers tell me that you performed brave and noble deeds in delivering them from the evil of the White-Eyes," El Mesias said. "And as I look at you I cannot tell if you are a White-Eyes or not. There is something decidedly different about the way you dress and even speak. And I think your eyes betray Indian blood in your veins."

Tom's voice was cold. "Think what you wish."

"Your tone is unfriendly," El Mesias said calmly.

"No," Tanaka Tom replied. "It is disrespectful."

"Do not trifle with me, Cuchillo Largo," El Mesias said. "Do you know the meaning of my name?"

"I know the translation of *el mesias*," Tom answered. "That is Spanish for messiah. But that is not your name."

"And Cuchillo Largo is not yours, White-Eyes," El Mesias answered.

"I advise you to employ the pronoun 'sir' when you speak to me," Tom said, laying his hand on the hilt of the *katana*.

"I'll ask for the same courtesy then," El Mesias said. "If you insist on being facetious."

"You are obviously an educated man," Tom said. "Your speech indicates that. What I don't understand is why someone with so superior an intellect and great leadership potential for his people, would take them down such a disastrous and stupid path to destruction."

"*I* do nothing, Cuchillo Largo," the Indian said. "It is Thunder Eagle who speaks through me and I am merely an implement of his bidding."

Brujo, the medicine man, could stand no more of this talk. "Liar! Crazy man! The great god Thunder Eagle spits on you. You are—"

The nearest guard's lance struck out stabbing the old man in the side, and immediately Tom's *katana* flew from its scabbard and sent the attacker's head to the ground. The second guard made a quick move toward Tom, then immediately stumbled back with both hands gone, but still clutching the lance where they lay in the dirt. Tom raised his sword and cut the hapless man from shoulder to waist in a quick but easy slice. The body tumbled to El Mesias' feet. The Indian, unshaken, looked down on the hunks of meat that once made up his two bodyguards.

"Your skill with the sword has been related to me many times," he said. "Now I know all those stories were true."

"Would you test my blade?"

"Perhaps. But not now. Thunder Eagle may decide to with his lightning, and that will be the end of Cuchillo Largo," El Mesias said. "It is true you can defeat most men with your speed and sharp blade, but you are not an Indian—no matter what ceremonies you have participated in—and that will be your death warrant as it is to all White-Eyes in this land."

"By Apache custom I am a member of this clan without any exceptions," Tanaka Tom said. "And I claim all the rights and privileges of that law."

"Very good," El Mesias answered. "You shall have those benefits, and the responsibilities too. Such as the obligation to obey Thunder Eagle completely and blindly."

"When he speaks to me, I shall obey," Tom agreed.

"Then heed my voice, Cuchillo Largo, for it is Thunder Eagle speaking through me."

"I refuse to accept that," Tom said.

"Then you are *not* an Apache and you must suffer the consequences," El Mesias said. He turned to the band of warriors. "Know this then! The man you call Cuchillo Largo is no longer an Apache. Thunder Eagle has stripped that honor from him as he would eagle feathers from a buzzard. To obey and follow him or his counsel is to die and spend eternity in the dark bowels of the earth as will all Apaches who believe not in Thunder Eagle and his power. Therefore, if you are true members of the Ancha Mesa clans, come with me. We leave this place and go forth to punish the White-Eyes . . . then the Mexicans . . . then other Indians who are enemies of our people."

Lagarto, caught up in the spirit of the moment, raised his lance high and emitted a long howl. "Let us travel the glory path with El Mesias and Thunder Eagle! When this land is ours again, we shall live and hunt unmolested by the evil of outsiders and other clans."

"Don't go, Thunder Eagles," Tom said. "Remember who gave birth to your society . . . me! Remember who led you against the soldiers and won . . . Osote, Guerrero, and me! Remember it was us who kept both the Valbajos and Montaltas here on the Ancha Mesa."

"Things have changed, Cuchillo Largo," Lagarto sneered. "And your medicine is diminishing even as Thunder Eagle's and El Mesias' grows."

"My power is in my sword, Lagarto," Tom said angrily. He had endured more in insulting behavior than *bushido* allowed, and he felt a compulsion to let his sword drink more blood that day. "Would you care to test it?"

"I will!" a young brave suddenly cried.

"And I!" another echoed.

"Me too," another shouted.

The three rushed past Lagarto and charged Tom with

their lance heads aimed dead on his chest. The samurai twisted deftly as he pulled the *katana* from its scabbard. He spun again and went between two of the lances as he raised the sword above his head. One downward stroke and the youngster on the far right fell in two heaps of twisting meat. The middle Apache turned in time to catch a strong thrust that drove the *katana* blade upward through his abdomen and into his lungs. He staggered back with pinkish blood bubbling from his lips before he collapsed.

The third warrior was able to charge once more. Tom waited for him, and the instant before contact grasped the Apache's right arm and slipped to his knee sending the brave flying over his head. Before his opponent could recover he found Tom's *katana* against his throat.

The samurai looked at El Mesias. "What would you have me do with him?"

"Kill him, if it pleases you. Thunder Eagle will send his spirit back to make war as a shadow," El Mesias said.

Tom looked down on the Apache. "What do you say now, *joven?*"

"I am ready to die," the brave said defiantly.

"Then it is your *karma*," Tanaka Tom said. The sword blade flew up and back in a flash. The victim's head simply rolled a foot or two away from his body. The samurai shouted toward El Mesias, "Because of you I have been an instrument of death for a brave man who was a Thunder Eagle. I will not forgive you that."

El Mesias laughed. "Then we are at war, Thomas Fletcher."

"Any battle with you will be but one of many I have experienced," Tom said.

"But you will not fight me alone," El Mesias said, gesturing toward the Thunder Eagle society. "These warriors are mine . . . *mine!*"

"Listen to me," Tom said to the crowd of braves. "This man brings the death and destruction of the Ancha Mesa clans. Your proven leaders Osote and Guerrero know the best path to follow."

"Too late," El Mesias cried. Then he flung back his head and began laughing—softly at first, but soon he was cackling as if hysterical, the sounds echoing off the hills around them. "Come, Thunder Eagles! We leave the Ancha Mesa now and go forth to destroy the interlopers who defile the sacred lands of our ancestors."

The assembled Apaches let out a loud war cry and, as one, surged forward toward their leader. They brushed past Tanaka Tom and trampled their dead comrades' bodies as they gathered around El Mesias.

"If you leave, the people who stay behind will be helpless before your enemies," Tom said. "With so few fighting men left it will be impossible to defend even this place."

"He is a weeping old woman!" El Mesias shouted. "No one would dare come here once the wrath of Thunder Eagle strikes. His words are as empty as shattered water gourds."

"You have enemies in Mexico and in the White-Eyes' army who are waiting for a chance to massacre your people. And you will die under the leadership of this *loco*. His medicine is false and impotent."

"Why can't you see the truth, Cuchillo Largo?" Lagarto asked. "There has been much evidence of El Mesias' power. We have seen him change when Thunder Eagle takes over his body. Ride with us! Be an Apache!"

"Apache or samurai," Tanaka Tom said. "I will not follow a fool."

Lagarto sneered in anger. "And I will not be the friend of one. I shall go with El Mesias."

"And so will they all!" El Mesias shouted. He gestured at the members of the Ancha Mesa warrior society. "Follow me, *mis valientes*, we shall perform the dictates and will of our god Thunder Eagle!"

Tom kept his *katana* ready for any sneak attack as the young leader ushered his charges out of the clearing. But no one made any hostile moves and within moments Tanaka Tom stood alone. Only after the warriors had definitely vacated the area did he move down toward the village to seek out Osote and Guerrero. Even as he strode through the wickiups, he could see evidence

41

that the Apaches' fighting strength had been more than decimated. He felt a deep foreboding, and even if he did not know for sure about Chaparro's gang or MacNally's squadron, he could sense the danger closing in on the Ancha Mesa.

Chapter Five

Ernesto Martinez eased through the vegetation, then stopped short at the sight of the Apache boy standing guard. Martinez, leader of a scouting party from Chaparro's gang of *bandidos,* had spent considerable time leading his six-man team up through the woods of the Ancha Mesa on the spy mission his chief had given him. He turned back to the other bandits and silently signaled them to halt. Then he pointed to one of the men and motioned him to crawl forward.

The other bandit, a short, swarthy individual named Tomas, with an enormous moustache filled with the debris of several meals, joined Martinez. *"¿Qué pasa?"* he asked.

"A little *guardia* blocks our way," Martinez said softly. "The situation calls for your *especialidad.*"

Tomas nodded with an evil grin that revealed a neglected set of rotting teeth. He pulled back then disappeared into the brush off to one side as Martinez waited. He could see the Apache boy, absent-mindedly scratching a brown buttock, as he kept a close vigil on a nearby trail. Martinez had no time to grow impatient. Tomas appeared instantly and silently behind the boy. He took only enough time to nod back toward Martinez before he clapped his hand over the boy's mouth and drove his knife under the youth's rib cage and up into the vital organs. The brief struggle was silent, then the Apache was lowered into his own blood that now formed a pool in the leaves at his feet.

Martinez turned back to the rest of his group. *"Vámanos.*

Let's go.'' The mission he led was an auxilliary one meant to be but a brief survey of the Apache's home camp on the Ancha Mesa. While Chaparro organized his forces for a full scale war, he wanted to have at least a quick peek at his adversaries.

Like his subordinate Tomas, Martinez had been chosen for this job because of his peculiar talents. He was one of the best scouts in Chaparro's band. He had learned the craft during time spent with his mother's people—the feared Yaqui Indians of Sonora. During his reconnaissances he was a perfectionist. He permitted none of the flashy dress most *bandidos* favored. The huge *sombreros* were left back with the horses. In their places the scouting party wore dark-colored bandanas around their heads Indian fashion. They also sported plain clothing of somber shades and carried only the essential ammunition and weapons needed. Their heavy cartridge belts, which they preferred to wear, crossed over their shoulders, had been left with the headgear. Before ascending the Ancha Mesa, Martinez had made each man jump up and down to make sure there would be no jangling or jingling of weapons, equipment or other items on their persons. When Ernesto Martinez wanted *silencio*, he didn't fool around.

Tomas, the knife killer, had to be sent forward one more time to eliminate a young sentry, before the small party of Mexicans gained the top of the mesa and were able to actually view the Apache village.

"How long do we stay here?" one *bandido* asked.

"Long enough to watch these *indios* and determine what they are doing," Martinez answered. "I am going to post you filthy *cabrónes* at various points of observation. I want you to stay quiet but awake. If I catch any *hijo de la chingada* sleeping, I'll kick his *nalgas* up between his ears."

After positioning his party of spies, Martinez settled into his own chosen spot and began a long period of patiently watching the Ancha Mesa Apaches going about their business. He knew he didn't have much time. Before long the dead boys would be discovered, then those *diablos* of

Apaches would begin scouring every inch of the Ancha Mesa to discover the killers.

But Ernesto Martinez didn't need much time.

The village was obviously badly understrength in warriors. The men of fighting age had either already gone to war or were out on a hunting party. It didn't matter which. The fact that they were gone became overwhelmingly apparent to even the slowest witted of the bandits. After a couple of hours, Martinez signaled his men to withdraw from the spy posts and assemble with him some distance down the hill.

Tomas, the quiet killer, shook his head. "Where are the *guerreros*—the warriors?"

Martinez shrugged. "Who knows or cares? But it looks like we have a chance for some fun . . . and a little profit too."

One of the other bandits, a weasel-faced individual named Chavez, looked up alarmed. "What do you have in mind, Martinez?"

"I thought we might pull a quick raid and perhaps nab a scalp or two off those *indios*."

Tomas shook his head violently. "Are you *loco?* Chaparro told us to avoid contact with the Apaches. We were to only spy on them, *verdad?*"

"Of course," Martinez said. "But he didn't know the village was practically empty of fighting men, did he?"

Chavez echoed Tomas' doubts. "I don't want to get into trouble with Chaparro. Going before a firing squad is not my idea of the best way to begin a day."

Martinez laughed. "*¡Mujeres!* Women! Don't be afraid. If I give the order to attack, then I alone will be responsible."

"That's true," Chavez said. "But why take a chance?"

"For pesos, *idiota!*" Martinez spat. "We can sell what scalps we take to the *Rurales* on our way back."

Tomas scuffed one boot in the dirt thoughtfully. "I don't know. . . ."

"*¡Ay, chingado!*" Martinez swore. "I'm not taking any votes. I've made a decision of command, *comprenden?* Now get back to your original posts. When I think the time is right I will fire my *pistola*. Then we all rush in and kill the nearest Apaches. Tomas and I will do the scalping while you others cover us. Any questions? Then move your *nalgas, pronto!*"

Martinez checked his Colt .45 as he watched his men scramble back up the hill to their positions. When he was satisfied they had resettled themselves, he struggled up the slope to his own observation post. The Apaches still maintained their lethargic routine, and the dearth of warriors remained.

The *bandido* took careful aim on a nearby squaw and fired. She bucked and whirled under the impact of the bullet before collapsing to the ground. Martinez leaped through the brush and charged into the village as his men did likewise on either side of him. Several more women and a child fell in the shower of slugs as Tomas joined Martinez and the two rushed to the nearest bodies to begin their bloody work.

But a sudden glance froze Martinez' blood.

Two Apaches and a strange man had suddenly made an appearance from the wickiups. All three were firing carbines, but there was something about the non-Indian that sent spasms of fear and uncertainty through Martinez' being. This man was dressed strangely with a wide sash around his middle. Two sticks, one rather long and the other much shorter, were stuck in the device. Two of the bandits collapsed to the dirt as the three carbineers let loose several volleys at the Mexicans. Martinez, about ready to leap to his feet and flee, stopped when he noted one of his men edging around a wickiup and position himself behind the Apaches and their friend.

But the strange man suddenly seemed to sense the danger to the rear and he spun in an instantaneous motion that ended with one of the "sticks" held high in both hands. Martinez thought he must have blinked his eyes to miss the action, but even as his mind perceived that the thing in the man's grasp was a sword, the instrument slashed down and cleaved the unfortunate bandit to his waist. Just as quickly the blade was withdrawn and once again whistled in the air—this time in a horizontal stroke. The bandit's head leaped from his shoulders and, along with the mutilated body, hit the dust of the Ancha Mesa village.

Martinez, Tomas and Chavez fled from the strange apparition that moved like lightening.

* * *

Dancing flames lit the sides of Tanaka Tom Long Knife's wickiup as he, Osote and Guerrero sat around the small fire in front of the structure.

Osote idly tossed a pebble into the blaze. "It seems the *mexicanos* are buying our hair again."

"All on account of that *perrito* El Mesias," Guerrero said. "His arrival on the Ancha Mesa heralded a situation worse than before. At least then we could have hidden in Mexico."

"We still can," Osote said. "Provided we go to our place in the Duro Mountains."

"That would only delay the certainty of our destruction," Guerrero remarked angrily.

Tanaka Tom sipped the tea that Paloma had brewed for him in accordance with his strict instructions. "What is this place in the Duro Mountains you are speaking of? This is in Mexico, is it not?"

"Yes," Osote answered. "It is a place our people have used as a refuge for many, many years. But it is hard to live there, Cuchillo Largo. Water is scarce and there is hardly any game. The only occassions the Ancha Mesa Apaches have fled there were during our worst and most desperate times.

"It can be a terrible place," Guerrero said. "Only small hunting parties stop there now. The springs there dry up after only a few have drunk from them. It takes a day— sometimes two or three—for them to fill up again."

Tanaka Tom nodded. "That would account for the scarcity of game then." He sat in thought for several long moments. "Tell me something, brothers, how long could the people here last in that Duro Mountain retreat?"

Osote shrugged. "Maybe a long time if we waited for the last one to die. But in order to bring out as many people as we take in there, we could only stay one moon."

46

"*Sí,*" Guerrero said in agreement. "*Una luna,* no more."

"This calls for deep thought," Tanaka Tom said.

"Is your mind churning up ways for us to solve these problems that El Mesias has rained down on us?" Osote asked.

"I hope so," the samurai said. He suddenly remembered the veteran officer Taguchi who had served in the Fujika *Rentai,* the elite unit of the Shogun's in whose ranks Tanaka Tom had also fought. Taguchi hated static warfare. He reveled in the bloody ebb and flow of open fighting where maneuver could be employed prior to the deadly clash of samurai warriors. Once, after a particularly bloody siege in which the Fujika Rentai had stormed a rebellious *daimyo's* castle and rendered its garrison into a smashed remnant of its former self, he had pointed out the horror of defending an unmovable area. "Your enemy has the whole world in which to feed and supply himself," he had told young Tom Fletcher. "But behind walls you must fight, while trying to draw strength and sustenance from an ever dwindling supply. Only a fool barricades himself, Tanaka Ichimara Tomi, a wise samurai seeks his glory in the open." Tom pondered the warrior's advice for a while, then decided Taguchi had left out the one thing that being behind walls can many times earn: *time!* And, at that particular moment, the Ancha Mesa Apaches needed that commodity badly.

"Can the place in the Duro Mountains be defended?" he asked.

Osote nodded. "Yes, easily. Much better than here on the Ancha Mesa, Cuchillo Largo."

"Only small teams of enemy could penetrate the defenses there," Guerrero said. "But such tactics work almost anywhere else as well."

"I am thinking of going there," Tom said. "What if we had to stay more than a month?"

"The weak would die first, of course," Osote said. "But it would be just as I said. Less people would come down from those mountains than went up there."

"The weak that couldn't survive would include the

47

children," Guerrero reminded him. "And that would include your own son Pumito."

"If that is his *karma* then nothing can prevent it," Tanaka Tom said. "But we need time."

"Time for what?" Osote asked. "El Mesias will have increased his evil a great deal within a moon. Time seems our enemy."

"No," Tom said. "If we take the people to the safety of the Duro Mountains, then we can approache the American authorities and convince them that only a small portion of the Ancha Mesa Apaches are guilty of the crimes being committed."

Guerrero spat. "*¡Mierda!* The White-Eyes will not listen to us. Remember their justice almost caused the three of us here to lose our lives. Only a miracle delivered us."

Tanaka Tom shook his head in disagreement. "No. The boy I saved from being tortured by you spoke out the truth in gratitude. It was that simple act of freeing him that brought about a great victory."

"Ah, Cuchillo Largo," Osote said. "You are telling us that sometimes great medicine is made from little deeds."

"Exactly," the samurai said. "Even though most of the Ancha Mesa warriors are following El Mesias, we might start a chain of events rolling that would deliver them back to us in time to save their lives."

"And if they don't return?" Osote asked.

Tom gestured to the wickiups around them. "Then at least we can save these people here. Do you want to go on a reservation?"

"I would rather die!" Osote exclaimed.

"We might anyway," Guerrero said.

"If it is destined, then it will happen," Tanaka Tom said. "But in the meantime I prefer to take action to prevent any calamities or disasters from overtaking us."

"Then let us take these people to the Duro Mountains," Guerrero said.

"It will be difficult and dangerous," Osote reminded them both. "The *mexicanos* will hunt us as if we are animals."

"Then the sooner we leave, the sooner we will have

passed the danger,'' Tanaka Tom said. ''I suggest we begin preparations immediately.''

Osote sighed and stood up. ''*Está bien,* Cuchillo Largo. I only hope this *karma* of which you speak looks on us favorably.''

The Six-gun Samurai's face was expressionless. ''We will soon know.

* * *

The faint red rays of the dawning sun gently bathed the war camp as El Mesias gradually awoke from the deep slumber that engulfed his being during the two hours he generally slept out of every twenty-four.

He sat up and rubbed his eyes, letting the cool air bring his state of wakefulness to full birth. Then he stood—not as El Mesias the War Leader—but as Solomon Sonador, an educated and intelligent young Indian man. He looked around the camp at the blanketed figures of sleeping warriors and noted the lookouts at their posts; alert and watchful despite the early hour.

His head ached fretfully and he squinted his eyes against the pain until it subsided to a dull throbbing. Solomon hated this particular time of day. His mind was lucid, ready to ponder any problem or difficulty with clear, open logic. The only trouble he experienced was in trying to recall what had taken place twenty-four hours before.

This situation had been occurring for the previous ten years, the first time being as a student at the Strong Oak Indian Academy. For two terrifying hours his mind was a complete blank. He couldn't remember where he was or who he was as he stumbled through the darkened dormitory of sleeping students in a blind panic. Finally someone grabbed him and spoke soothing words into his ear. The event had been passed off as an ''attack of nerves'' by the local physician, but three months later it happened again . . . then once more in one month's time . . . after that only a week's respite relieved the horrible moments of nothingness. Finally it was a daily thing when the frightening period of amnesia locked him into a vacuum of horrible nothingness.

49

But things didn't really get bad until Lucie Devlin.

Lucie's father, Professor Horace Devlin, served as a senior member of the faculty at Strong Oak Indian Academy. In addition to his post as an instructor in moral and religious philosophy, he acted as counselor to various students. One of those assigned to him had been Solomon Sonador. The young Apache, because of his disturbing mental state, sought the professor's guidance and advice on numerous occassions. Their contacts became so frequent that many an evening, sitting in front of the fireplace in Devlin's modest home, the two would talk far into the night. A firm friendship seemed to be in the making between the older white man and this youth who had come straight out of a near stone-age existence. Then Lucie began sitting in on their sessions.

Solomon was at first flustered by Lucie's presence. She was a strikingly pretty girl only a year or two younger than he. Honey blonde with blue eyes, she was a direct opposite of the Indian girls he had known. She also displayed a directness in her gaze that unnerved him to some extent. At first he saw her only during his visits to the Devlin residence, but later on they would meet, as if by chance, at various times on campus.

These meetings evolved into short, then longer conversations; then into innocent rendezvous in the quieter areas of the academy grounds. Finally these planned encounters moved from places where they could be seen to hidden spots in the woods around the school.

Then the inevitable happened.

Solomon, still an Apache several years past the normal time for sexual activity, arrived at one of their clandestine encounters carrying the one item he still had from his former days on the Ancha Mesa—a blanket.

Lucie sensed something different in his attitude. His handsome face bore an expression that rendered her powerless in its intensity. He knelt beside her and slid the blanket over her shoulders, then he moved beneath the cover also.

"Solomon?" she had asked with a hint of uncertainty in her voice.

50

"You will be my woman," Solomon said firmly.

Lucie swallowed hard and smiled weakly but did not pull away. "I don't understand what you want."

Centuries of Apache tradition and instincts came to the fore as Solomon reached out and stroked her cheek. "There is nothing for you to understand, Lucie. You will do as I want you to."

"Yes, Solomon."

He slid his hand under her skirt, probing against the unfamiliar barriers of lace, silk and other fabric. An Apache girl back home would have been naked and open under her buckskin dress, her feminity ready to receive whatever attention her lover cared to render.

Solomon pushed her back until Lucie lay in the grass. Then he raised her skirt, his excitement growing at the sight of the pale, smooth thighs above the black stockings. He reached under her chemise and grasped the bulky underdrawers and pulled them down and off.

Lucie, though uncertain, did nothing to resist as the Apache settled himself between her legs, his trousers now down around his knees as his manhood strained to the front as if a war lance made of flesh. He pushed it against her torso, and she cried out but once before he slid into her now bleeding interior. Then the savage took over his being and he ravished the girl in a rage-love emotionally charged rape until he grunted in triumph when he ejaculated as a final gesture of triumph and victory.

Lucie cried a little as she rearranged her clothing, but by the time she was able to stand, the girl had completely recovered. She smoothed her skirt and gave Solomon one final look before leaving. "I'll see you tomorrow as usual . . . here."

From that moment on the two met several times a week, as Lucie bit her lip and endured the strange pleasure of pain the Indian youth inflicted on her. Solomon by then was becoming confused as to how to continue the courtship. His primitive instincts were beginning to collide with the subtler notions of civilized romance his exposure to the white man's literature taught him. Finally he broached his confusion to Lucie who knew exactly what to say:

"You must go to papa and ask his permission to marry me."

Solomon agreed that this seemed to be the accepted custom and on the next visit to Professor Devlin's house he calmly asked for Lucie's hand. Her father's reaction surprised, shocked, and hurt him deeply.

Horace Devlin, while perfectly happy to work with Indians and teach them—even be friends, if necessary— was not about to have one marry into his family. His liberalism ended at his front doorstep and no other man but one who could boast of one hundred per cent European stock was going to wed his daughter.

Solomon was turned out of the house, Lucie was sent away to live with an old maid aunt in Boston and the warm relationship that had existed between teacher and student came to an abrupt and final cessation.

But a new, shadowy being entered Solomon Sonador's world to fill in the gap of rejection and affrontery—*Thunder Eagle!*

The legend of this Apache god floated in the darkest recesses of Solomon's memory. And the emotional upheaval of the severed love affair triggered an increase in his growing insanity. During one of his deepest periods of delusion, Thunder Eagle made his first appearance and spoke to him.

"You are not Solomon Sonador," the apparition told him. "You are a Hawk of Lightning, which is a bearer of my messages and my will to the clans of the Apache nation. I will visit you many times to tell you who you truly are and what you must do. And, when the time is right, I will inform you of your true name, which will explain your purpose in serving both Spirit Woman and me."

Now, several years later, having adopted the name that came from the twisted world of his lunacy, El Mesias knew that for some reason he stood in the center of a primitive camp. He could recall the previous period of wakefulness, and it had been in the Ancha Mesa village (which he remembered from childhood), but what occurred between those times of consciousness was as lost to him as if he had never existed. But Solomon knew he was involved in some sort of unusual activity. His genius could not be stifled or fooled by confusion or ignorance of events. What tortured his superlative intellect was not *knowing* what he was doing or why. And the varying patterns of his environment added to his confusion.

The headache began to gradually increase until the intensity was unbearable. He sank to his knees with his hands clasped tightly to his skull as the pounding increased to the staccato of a war drum. Then suddenly it ceased. The pain was gone and a new feeling of strength and vitality flowed through his body. He looked up and saw the tall feathered giant of Thunder Eagle standing before him.

"Hawk of Lightning," Thunder Eagle said. "Do my bidding."

El Mesias, his eyes aflamed with righteous fervor, suddenly scampered among the sleeping forms of the warriors kicking them awake in an insane dance.

"Thunder Eagles, awake! Get your weapons and ponies ready, today we begin our crusade and we follow our Apache gods on the warpath to destroy all other men of this world!"

Chapter Six

Chaparro scratched his unshaven chin and looked skeptically into Martinez' face. "How many Apaches attacked you?"

"So many I could not count them, *Jefe*," Martinez lied with a weak smile. "But it wasn't the Indians that defeated us. It was the madman with the swords."

"¿Qué?" Chaparro asked. "You are telling me that somebody with swords went up against your gunmen and beat you?"

"Yes, *Jefe*," Martinez said. "He had a long one and a short one. And a carbine too. But he killed more with the blades than the gun."

Chaparro lit a cigar taking his time as he expelled the smoke. Then his gaze bored into Martinez' own eyes. "You are confusing me. For the past twenty minutes you have been rambling about a surprise attack on you by an overwhelming number of Ancha Mesa Apaches. Yet reliable sources tell me the majority of warriors from that village are away making war. Somebody is lying to me, Martinez. Is it you?"

Martinez' lips trembled. "*¡Que no, Jefe!* I am telling the truth. I swear on my sainted mother's grave."

Chaparro spat. "Your mother was a whore and still lives, so spare me your pious pledges of veracity. Truth has never been one of your passions, Martinez."

"Perhaps not," Martinez admitted. "But when strange things happen, even a priest is hard pressed to impress others that what he relates is not false."

"Very well," Chaparro said. "But I want to hear more about this *diablo* who prefers swords to guns. What magic did he work that made him so invincible?"

"It was the magic of speed, *Jefe*," Martinez said. "In the wink of an eye he could turn completely around and dump heads into the dirt with his flying blade. He was a blur of rapid movement. How can one take aim on such a man, *Jefe*?"

Chaparro shook his head. "I must speak to others about this *espada*—this swordsman. Who else survived this devil's curse?"

Martinez hesitated. The last thing he wanted was for others to relate what had happened to his patrol up on the Ancha Mesa. "Nobody of importance, *Jefe*."

"Are you suggesting their verbal skills do not match your own?" Chaparro asked.

Martinez brightened. "Correct, *Jefe*. They are too inarticulate to relate the incident to you in terms worthy or accurate enough for your ears."

"I hate Apaches," Chaparro said softly. "I hate *gringos* too . . . also women who talk too much. But I do not hate

54

them as much as I hate some *hijo de la chingada* who insults my intelligence, Martinez. Who were the survivors of this fight you are telling me about?"

"Well, *Jefe . . .*" Martinez scuffed the dirt with the tip of his boot. "There was . . . let me think. . . ."

Chaparro drew his revolver in one smooth rapid move and aimed it dead on Martinez' face. "Who survived that battle?"

"Tomas and Chavez," Martinez answered quickly.

Chaparro turned to a nearby bandit. "Fetch them. *pronto!*"

Martinez smiled weakly and tried to whistle nonchalantly, but his lips were too dry. He swallowed hard a couple of times before he spoke again. "You need me any more, *Jefe?*"

"*Stay where you are!*" Chaparro shouted.

"*Por su puesto*—of course," Martinez said in a low, respectful voice.

By then Tomas and Chavez were issued into the august presence of their gang leader. Each stood smiling, holding his sombrero in front of him as a gesture of respect.

Chaparro looked at the closest one. "Who are you?"

"I am called Tomas, *Jefe.*"

"Very well, Tomas, tell me what happened to you and your friends up on the Ancha Mesa," Chaparro commanded.

"Gladly, *mi jefe,*" Tomas answered. Then he quickly recited the story of the attack on the village that was made because there were no great number of warriors present.

"You were not attacked then?" Chaparro asked.

"No, *Jefe.* We charged into the village," Tomas said. Then he frowned at Martinez. "We thought we might get some scalps to sell on our way back here."

"Then no large group of warriors defeated you and ran you off?" Chaparro asked.

"No," Tomas answered. "There were not too many fighting men in the village."

Martinez groaned.

Chaparro glanced at the other bandit. "And what is your name?"

"I am called Chavez."

"I want to hear your version of the attack on the Ancha Mesa Apaches."

Chavez repeated the story almost word-for-word. Once again Martinez' anguish was evident.

Chaparro nodded. "What about this fellow with the sword?"

Both Tomas and Chavez began talking at the same time, so their chief ordered them to become silent. He pointed to Tomas. "You tell me."

"He was a *diablo*—a devil!" Tomas said. "I have never in all my life seen a man who could move so fast. Heads flew, *mi jefe*, as he spun like a tornado."

"His blades flashed like lightning!" Chavez added. "It was as if he were some sort of demon from hell. We fled from him, *Jefe*. Nobody could stand up against him. And he had a carbine too. Whoever he aimed it at died as well."

"I am fascinated by this creature," Chaparro said. "It seems probable that our little family will meet him again."

"And I will point him out to you, *Jefe*," Martinez said hopefully.

"¡*Idiota*!" Chaparro exclaimed. "How could I miss such a phenomenon? Besides you won't be around to do anything."

"What are you talking about, *Jefe*?" Martinez asked in a voice filled with apprehension.

Chaparro turned to two of his bodyguards that always stood close to him. "Take Martinez' weapons," he told them. Then as the hapless *bandido* was roughly disarmed, Chaparro pronounced sentence on him. "You are to be shot immediately."

"For losing a battle to a supernatural enemy?" Martinez asked.

"For disobeying my orders and lying to me," Chaparro said angrily. "You were told not to attack the village. Only to scout and spy on them."

Martinez hung his head. "You are right, *Jefe*. I deserve nothing better."

Chaparro looked at Tomas. "Gather up his friends and bring them here."

"My woman too," Martinez said. He looked at Chaparro and shrugged. "I would like to say *adíos*, you understand, *Jefe*."

"Of course," Chaparro said. "It is only proper."

Within fifteen minutes several people, including a weeping woman, stood around the condemned man. Martinez wasted no time in passing out his meager possessions. His guns went to one grateful acquaintance who shed crocodile tears while accepting his "inheritance." The horse went to another *bandido* who was clearly not too pleased with the wretched animal. After various watches and other paraphernalia of countless robberies were passed out, Martinez called to Tomas.

"What do you have for me?" Tomas asked eagerly.

"You have always been a great help to me," Martinez said. "Your skill in silent killing with the knife has been the cause of many successful scouts. Therefore I want you to have my most prized possession—my woman Sofia."

Tomas looked at the fat, big breasted woman with undisguised lust. "*Muchas gracias*, Martinez."

Sofia wailed, "But I do not like him. He smells bad and I've seen him beat girls."

Martinez cuffed her ear not too gently. "*¡Callate!*—shut up! Cook his food and satisfy his needs like a good *bandido*'s woman without complaints. Who cares how he smells?"

Chaparro was growing impatient. "Hurry up! A *millonario* could dispose of his estates in less time than it is taking you to pass out a few miserable baubles and a used-up woman."

"I'm sorry, *Jefe*, excuse me," Martinez said. "Now I am ready."

Chaparro nodded to his bodyguards. "Do the job."

Martinez walked a ways off. "Will somebody do me a favor?" he called back to his friends. "If you ever come across a church, light a candle for me, eh?"

"I'll do it," Tomas said with his arm around Sofia's ample waist.

"*Gracias, amigo*," Martinez said. Then he looked at

57

the gunmen who were taking aim. "*Estoy listo*—I am ready."

The shots echoed off the distant foothills as Martinez crumpled to the sand. Chaparro himself walked up and delivered the *coup de gráce* by placing his revolver barrel in Martinez' ear and pulling the trigger.

Then Chaparro shouted to Martinez' friends, "Everybody clear out! You have your things . . . and don't forget to take Martinez with you, eh? I don't want him rotting around here."

Tomas, Sofia, and Chavez went over to the dead *bandido* and dragged his corpse away from Chaparro's lodgings. As he watched them struggle away with their burden, the bandit chief sank deep into thought. This stranger with swords was fast becoming a legend among his men. If he were to maintain his leadership and reputation among his semi-savage followers, he would have to personally see that the strange *diablo* was destroyed—and the sooner the better.

* * *

A loud, continuous keening of anguished female voices floated over the Ancha Mesa. Paloma settled Pumito down on the blanket spread out in front of the wickiup door. The baby gurgled good-naturedly despite the miserable sounds permeating the area. "There is much sorrow, Cuchillo Largo," Paloma said.

Tanaka Tom turned from packing his belongings prior to loading them on the mule. "There will be hardships to be endured," he admitted. "But they are necessary if the people of the Ancha Mesa are to survive."

Paloma walked up beside the samurai. "Why do you not let me prepare your things for the journey?" she asked. "That is a squaw's duty."

"Many of the items here are delicate," Tanaka Tom said. "The method of transporting them involves containers and ways of putting things away you would not understand."

Paloma pouted. "And I suppose a Japanese woman would, eh?"

58

"Of course," Tanaka Tom said artlessly. "You take care of your things and the utensils for our wickiup. Leave my own to me."

"Yes, *hombre mio*," Paloma said.

Tom, his mind full of the countless details of the journey, looked up in annoyance at the sound of the crying women. "How long will this weeping continue?"

Paloma shrugged. "I do not know. Most of the squaws have no men with them. Their husbands have gone with El Mesias. Since they are not around to beat them into silence, I think those women will shed tears and scream until our return."

The Six-gun Samurai fondled his *katana*. "I could lay the scabbard of this sword across a few backsides," he said sullenly. "Perhaps that will earn us blessed silence."

"Your temper is rising," Paloma said. "It is not like you."

"I am used to dealing with soldiers," Tanaka Tom said. "To have women and children directly under my command is unnerving and frustrating. I don't quite know how to handle the situation."

"Then prepare yourself," Paloma said, glancing past him. "Here come several women to speak with you."

Tanaka Tom looked up and spotted a delegation of squaws approaching him. Usually docile toward men, these women had developed an uncharacteristic mood of defiance both from the dreaded move to the desolate Duro Mountains as well as the absence of their warrior husbands.

The group stopped on the other side of Tom's mule. One older woman named Juncal stepped forward from the group and pointed her finger at Paloma. "We would talk with your man."

Paloma nodded. "*Hombre mio*, these women—"

Tom, ignoring Apache protocol, didn't wait for Paloma to make a formal statement. He turned to Juncal. "What do you want?"

"The women of the Ancha Mesa have asked me to speak in their behalf, Cuchillo Largo," Juncal said respectfully. "They do not want to go to the place in the Duro Mountains."

59

"They must go," Tanaka Tom said. "It is for their own good."

"I have been to the Duro Mountains," Juncal said. "Once when I was a child we fled there. Even after all these years the memory of that terrible place invades my dreams and I wake up weeping sometimes."

"We hope to be there only a short time," Tanaka Tom said. "There will be dried meat to take with us. We will not starve."

"Dried meat without water can cause a long, lingering death," Juncal said truthfully. "I remember that too. There is not enough water, Cuchillo Largo. It is easier to die from starvation than thirst."

"If you do not go you will be at the mercy of soldiers and Mexican bandits," Tanaka Tom Long Knife said. "The Mexicans want your scalps to sell. The soldiers want to kill you. But before they do they will ravish you until you are too hurt to enjoy further. Then you will die. How is that compared to starvation or thirst?"

"We are not afraid," Juncal said. "Thunder Eagle will protect us here on the Ancha Mesa."

"If he will protect you on the Ancha Mesa, then he will protect you in the Duro Mountains," Tanaka Tom said. "You have nothing to lose either way, *verdad?*"

The logic of the samurai's remarks caused the squaws to murmur among themselves. But Juncal wasn't finished. "If our great war god doesn't want us to go, he will punish us by making our time in the Duro Mountains even worse than before."

"If Thunder Eagle wishes you to stay here," Tanaka Tom said, "he will not let me take you. After all, I am a mere man and he is a god."

Juncal, though not convinced entirely, decided the best way to handle the situation was to agree. "We will let Thunder Eagle show us the way then. We will obey your orders, Cuchillo Largo, but if Thunder Eagle appears we must switch our obedience to him."

"Well said," Tanaka Tom said. "And I, too, will give way to Thunder Eagle's wishes. That way none of us must bear a curse from his wrath."

"And we—"

"Enough!" Tanaka Tom shouted as he interrupted her. "I will not stand here listening to women prattle. If you don't leave now I shall beat you . . . every one!"

The Apache women retreated from his anger as the samurai strode from his wickiup looking for Osote and Guerrero. It took him several minutes to walk through the camp to the area where the two Apache leaders had established their wickiups. They stood up and greeted him with warm smiles.

"It appears we shall be able to leave at dusk," Tanaka Tom said.

"Yes," Osote agreed. "And when we reach the worst part of the desert it will be well into the night. The darkness will cloak us from heat as well as the prying eyes of our enemies."

Tom noticed a group of people squatting off to one side. "Who are they?" he asked. "Why are they not ready to go?"

"They are not going, Cuchillo Largo," Guerrero said.

"Why not? I thought it was agreed that everyone on the Ancha Mesa would leave."

"Of course," Osote said. "But we did not mean the old people."

Tanaka Tom was shocked. "You mean we are to leave the elderly here. At the mercy of soldiers and bandits?"

"It is our custom," Guerrero explained. "The old ones would slow us down, and they are useless. It is best they die here alone, rather than out on the desert or in the Duro Mountains where they might cause the death of others."

"I have learned to respect and revere the elders," Tanaka Tom said. "To leave them behind is more than I could bear in shame and grief."

"What would you have us do with them?" Osote asked. "Kill them ourselves?"

"Of course not!" Tanaka Tom said shocked. "But I want them to come along with us. I pledge these weaker ones my respect and my protection."

"Then you are creating more danger for your own safety, Cuchillo Largo," Guerrero protested. "What we

61

face calls for strength and agility. These useless ones have neither."

"I must serve them nevertheless," Tanaka Tom insisted.

"Then you will die!" Osote cried.

Tanaka Tom remained calm. "Only if it is my *karma*."

Osote was genuinely grieved. "Then, my dear friend, it is obvious even to me that death indeed is your fate in this undertaking we face."

* * *

The sergeant's boot landed heavily and squarely on the seat of the trooper's trousers. The cavalryman turned angrily and immediately cooled his temper when he spotted the husky NCO standing over him. The soldier smiled weakly. "Somethin' the matter, Sarge?"

"I tole you bastards to stay alert, didn't I?" the sergeant growled. "If as much as one of them miserable Apaches git past us I'm gonna have your hides nailed to the barracks wall, understand?"

The trooper smiled weakly. "Sure . . . sure, Sarge, I'll keep my eyes open all right."

"See that you do." The sergeant turned from the ambush site and walked back to the small command post set up some twenty yards to the rear. He walked up to his commanding officer and saluted sharply. "Sir, the men are positioned and ready."

Captain Terrance MacNally returned the military greeting. "Very good, Sergeant. You can relax a bit now. I suggest you get some coffee while you have the chance."

"Yes, Sir."

As the sergeant strode away, Lieutenant Richard Martin watched him. "Seems to be quite an efficient NCO."

"Yes, indeed, Mister Martin," MacNally said. "Men like Sergeant Stensland are the backbone of the regular army."

"He keeps the men hopping all right," Martin agreed.

"Stensland hates to see anyone just sitting around," MacNally said. "Many a time I've heard him holler out, 'Come on you slugs, get moving!' Takes a lot of pressure off us officers."

Martin looked around. "I noticed there are some remnants of burned out buildings here, Sir."

"This was once the Ancha Mesa Indian Agency," MacNally explained. "That devil Thomas Fletcher led those howling savages here and massacred a hundred or so people."

"Horrible!" Martin exclaimed.

"The real horror was his getting away with it through the legal manipulations and shenanigans of a shyster lawyer," MacNally said. "But we'll get those pagan bastards this time, Mister Martin, and it will be a glorious beginning to your military career."

"I appreciate that, Sir," Martin said enthusiastically. "But just who is this person Fletcher?"

"He was once a decent white man," MacNally said. "In fact he was a midshipman in the United States Navy when he went to Japan with Admiral Perry. But something happened to him over there. He got caught up with the Jappos and they twisted him and turned him until he had become a bloodthirsty savage just like them. He joined an assassin cult over there, Martin, and he likes to kill with a blade better than a firearm, like decent men. Simply murdering someone doesn't satisfy him, Martin. He isn't contented until he mutilates his victims . . . usually by beheading them."

"My God! No wonder he feels a kinship to these Apaches," Martin said.

"Indeed," MacNally said. "And that's why he must be destroyed if and when we run across him."

"I shall make his death a prime requisite, Sir," Martin said.

"See that you do."

Sergeant Stensland reappeared and reported in once again. "Sir, our scouting parties have returned with news. It seems there is a large body of Apaches moving down off the mesa toward our positions."

"Good!" MacNally said. "Maybe we can wrap this particular Apache war up, right here and now."

"That ain't all, Sir," Sergeant Stensland said. "They say there's a white man with 'em."

63

"Fletcher, by God!" MacNally cried. "It's got to be that demonic son of a bitch! C'mon, Martin, let's get up to the perimeter."

The captain hurried forward with the others following closely. When they reached their front lines, they settled in behind the heavy brush to wait.

Within a half hour the first Apaches appeared.

MacNally fairly quivered with excitement as he carefully noted each individual appearing on the trail in the fading late afternoon light. Finally his eyes widened and seemed to light up. "See that one there! The one wearing the sash with the two swords . . . goddammit, do you see him?"

"Yes, Sir," Martin answered. "The white man? Is that Fletcher?"

"It sure as hell is!" MacNally said. He drew his pistol and saber as he leaped to his feet. "Open fire, men," he shouted as loudly as he could. "And take aim on the white man riding the Morgan! He's the devil incarnate and, by God, it'll go down in history that this command destroyed him!"

Chapter Seven

Bullets splattered around Tanaka Tom Long Knife, some knocking the bark off trees, others sending leaves scattering and plowing up small furrows in the dirt where they narrowly missed him. The samurai wasted no time in wheeling his horse off the trail before plunging into the thicker underbrush with the wide-eyed pack mule following in astonishment and fear.

Within moments Osote joined him in the cover of the foliage. "Soldiers, Cuchillo Largo," he said breathing hard. "They are well situated and block our way."

"I was afraid the U.S. Army had already begun their

campaign against us," Tanaka Tom said. "Does it look like we can fight through them?"

"If the Thunder Eagles were with us, yes," Osota answered. "But we are too few. We would all be shot down before we even cleared the bottom of the trail."

"Then we must go back up the mesa," Tom said reluctantly. "Perhaps with time we can figure another way out of this."

"What if the soldiers follow, Tanaka Tom?" Osote asked. "We cannot prevent them from defeating us even up on top of the Ancha Mesa."

"The soldiers do not know the El Mesias has taken the bulk of warriors with him," Tom explained. "They think there are many more of us than there really are. Once they figure out we are weak, however, they will not hesitate to overwhelm us."

"Then time is our friend at this moment," Osote said.

"Yes," Tom agreed. "But we'll have to offer tremendous battle to give the impression we are many instead of but a few. Let us join the others and urge them on."

Osote smiled fiercely. "Aiyee! It will be good to battle our enemies with you again, Cuchillo Largo!"

Guerrero, nearly breathless from exertion, joined them. "There are too many for us, Cuchillo Largo," he said, echoing the conclusion his two friends had already reached.

"Get the women and children moving back up to the top of the mesa," Tom said. "The warriors must fight doubly hard to contain the soldiers and prevent immediate pursuit. Remember they think there are many more of us than there actually are."

The noncombatants, sensing the situation, had already begun the ascent. Burros and mules burdened with belongings were switched and kicked impatiently as they were turned around. The bewildered animals brayed their annoyance and bounded up the trail as the small boys in charge shouted and beat at them.

Meanwhile Tom had reached the bottom of the trail where the fighting was fiercest. He quickly positioned what few warriors he had to better concentrate their fire on the soldiers who had so far remained static.

65

"Don't take too much time to aim," the samurai instructed the Apaches. "What is needed now are many flying bullets to force their heads down. We do not want the soldiers maneuvering around too much and discovering our true strength."

The warriors responded to his orders by increasing their rate of fire to such an extent that the enemy's own shooting volume nearly died out for several moments before the officers and sergeants were able to regain control of their troops and end the ducking and dodging in order to once again get back into the fight.

Tanaka Tom knew the cavalrymen had to be contained for at least an hour in order to give the women and children enough time to get out of danger. It seemed an easy enough task at that moment, but one thought kept nagging at him. It wouldn't take too long for any efficient field commander to figure out he was facing a decidedly inferior force . . . unless energetic and daring methods were employed at great risk.

"Osote! Guerrero!" he called out.

"Yes, Cuchillo Largo," Osote said, joining him as Guerrero followed. "The barrel of my carbine is now too hot to touch. Soon, like all the others, it may begin to misfire."

"Another risk we face," Tanaka Tom Long Knife said.

"What is one more among many?" Guerrero asked with a grin.

Tanaka Tom smiled back. "Exactly! And I am about to add yet another. We cannot remain in these positions for much longer. Soon the soldiers will be able to count the guns firing at them. We must now move around. We will split up the warriors between you two and myself. We must rush back and forth, pausing only to fire two or three shots in order to give the impression that we are a greater force."

"This idea is worth the hazards it threatens," Osote said. "I shall operate to the east."

"And I the west," Guerrero offered.

"That leaves me the center around the trail," Tom said. "Let us begin immediately."

The Six-gun Samurai rounded up a dozen warriors and split them into four teams of three each. They began a dangerous game of movement and fire as they dodged about in the underbrush, pausing only long enough to fire several quick shots before scampering to other positions.

Tanaka Tom Long Knife realized he was too conspicuous to move around like the warriors. Once the troops had spotted him in several locations, they would guess the ploy being used against them. And from the amount of fire being directed against him, Tom knew he was the center of attention.

Three Ancha Mesa warriors crumpled beneath cavalry bullets before the samurai felt it the right time to withdraw from the scene. When the small group of fighters gathered at the base of the trail the other casualties they sustained were sadly noted.

"At least we've saved our women and children," Osote said, trying to console himself and the others.

Guerrero, however, was bitter. "And where were the brave El Mesias and the Thunder Eagles when the soldiers pressed us so cruelly? As usual it took Cuchillo Largo to save us."

"We can speak of these things later," Tanaka Tom said. "We must retreat back up the trail to the village. Despite careful planning we have gained absolutely nothing and we have lost several good fighting men in the bargain."

"If we don't reach the Duro Mountains we are as good as dead," Osote said.

"This situation is hopeless at this point," Guerrero said through clenched teeth. "Perhaps we should begin our death songs now. We may be speaking with Spirit Woman face-to-face before tomorrow morning dawns."

Tanaka Tom Long Knife nodded his agreement. "Even if we get safely off the Ancha Mesa, I fear the *karma* for many of us will be death very soon."

* * *

The officers stood in uneasy silence as Captain MacNally paced back and forth in front of them. "By damn!" he exclaimed. "I don't understand why that devil Fletcher didn't put up a better fight."

"Perhaps he's trying to draw us up that trail, Sir," one of the company commanders offered.

"Too obvious for that devious son of a bitch," MacNally said. "I've got to think this thing out. There's something damned peculiar here, and if we're not careful Fletcher'll have our heads stacked like cordwood after those heathen friends of his roast us alive."

Captain Terrance James MacNally was a forty-five-year-old veteran with over twenty-five years of service in the regular army. Unlike many of his fellow officers he did not enjoy the privileges of a West Point education. In fact, Terry MacNally had very little formal learning at all. He had been born on the Bowery to impoverished, ignorant Irish immigrant parents. A naturally bright boy, he had used his wits and fists to earn his own way from the age of seven. He found his niche in life as a newspaper boy—after winning a good corner location by fighting a half-dozen others for it—and it was this choice of jobs that proved a boon for him.

Saint Didicus Church where Father Brian O'Leary served was located directly across the street from where Terry peddled papers. The priest had watched as the wiry youngster became "king of the hill" and was the only lad pursuing the peculiar area of the journalistic profession there. Father O'Leary had taken to purchasing a copy of the *New York Times* on a daily basis and always managed to strike up a conversation with the boy. He liked the youth's bright eyes and inquiring mind and, when he found the boy had no regular place to sleep, offered him a spot in the attic of the parish house. That enabled Terry to earn a few extra pennies each week by doing some cleaning chores and other errands for the priest and his housekeeper.

This purely business arrangement formed into a friendship that soon evolved into lessons the naturally bright lad quickly picked up. With no strict scheduling, priest and newsboy progressed through reading, writing, arithmetic, a bit of literature and even Latin before Terry reached his eighteenth birthday. Then, knowing that civilian life offered very little to a poor young man with no diplomas, he enlisted in the army in 1848.

Once again his talent with his fists came into being in the rough and tumble barracks life of the old regulars, and he finished his first five-year hitch wearing the double yellow chevrons of a cavalry corporal. By the time he was in the third year of his second hitch, he was awarded another stripe and pulled his time as a sergeant. When the second hitch was up, he re-enlisted, but by then he had more ambition.

The army offered a chance for commissions to soldiers who could pass through several rigorous examinations designed to weed out the unsophisticated and dull-witted. Sergeant MacNally's company commander had enough respect and faith in the tough, intelligent NCO to recommend him as a candidate for commission.

For a full year he studied and worked hard as he appeared before numerous special boards, beginning with his regiment and progressing up through various military departments. Finally, immaculate in full dress uniform complete with plumed helmet, he went in front of the final panel of examiners and took a tough oral test during which the stern old-line officers sought to mentally and emotionally rip him to shreds. But three months later in the year 1860 he received his commission as Second Lieutenant of United States Cavalry.

He held that same rank when he went into the Civil War but came out a brevet major. When that conflict ended, the regular army was reduced and so was the rank of the many officers who stayed in. Terrance MacNally found himself a first lieutenant posted to a new cavalry regiment at Fort Bozie, Arizona Territory. He served faithfully and well until promoted to captain a year previous. But the episode with the Six-gun Samurai had gotten him that hated Letter-of-Reprimand and he was destined to remain a captain for the rest of his days.

Until this final chance presented itself.

Now, turning to his assembled officers, Captain MacNally had formed his plan in his mind. "Gentlemen," he said.

69

"I think Thomas Fletcher is leading a weakened band of Apaches. It is evident to me that the conduct of today's battle indicates he could not defeat us. Which leaves him but one course to follow if he still desires to withdraw from the Ancha Mesa. He must go down the other, more dangerous side. Therefore, we shall move over there and wait for his arrival on the desert floor. At that time, gentlemen, we will allow him to move out, away from the cover of his blessed mesa and we will destroy him and those filthy Apaches once and for all! Prepare your men for an immediate move."

The officers saluted and ran off to their respective commands. Bugles sounded *Boots-and-Saddles* as MacNally's squadron prepared for the final battle of the Ancha Mesa War.

* * *

The young warrior held the lantern high as he negotiated the steep, rocky trail. He had gotten the illumination device the year before during the attack on the illegal Indian Agency that had been established through bribery and political contacts by the notorious Colonel Edward Hollister, Tanaka Tom Long Knife's sworn enemy.

The light flickered badly, causing many shadows among the crags and crevices as the Apache inched his way downward. Each time he began to rush, he checked himself by stopping to take several deep breaths to steady his patience just as he would if he were stalking a deer or other game through the woods. Even this precaution failed him as his foot stepped on to what seemed to be a shadow on a rock—instead it was nothingness, and the warrior tripped, his balance gone, and he floated in the black nothingness as wind whipped all around him.

He was able to sing his death song three full times before his body crashed into the boulders hundreds of feet below the mesa top.

"Cuchillo Largo!" Osote called out. "Another pathfinder is lost."

"I will take his place, Cuchillo Largo," Guerrero offered. "These youngsters hurry too much."

70

"No," Tanaka Tom said. "It is best to use a very young man. Their feet are surer and they have more agility."

Guerrero shook his head. "Already there are three smashed corpses on the rocks down there. Let me try, Cuchillo Largo."

"If I must lose you, old friend," Tanaka Tom said, "let it be at my side in battle. Not over a mountainside."

A young man rushed forward eagerly. "I, too, have a lantern from the old agency. Let me lead us down the trail to safety. I will not slip, Cuchillo Largo, I promise!"

"Very well," Tanaka Tom said. "Bring me your light and I will put fire in it."

The Apaches, while knowing the purpose of the lanterns, had never figured out how to use them properly, but they had enough native intelligence to figure out the supply of wicks and kerosene at the agency was part of the overall package. When it was decided to move off the mesa after dark, dozens of the instruments and gallons of the fuel had been produced from the wickiups.

The people, with the elders bringing up the rear, were strung out single file down the craggy, narrow path as the village population inched downward toward the desert floor. The children, like all Apache youngsters, were trained to endure hardship and inconvenience in silence and except for an occasional hungry baby they remained silent.

Tanaka Tom, expecting the cavalrymen to appear at their backs any time, had established a strong rear guard. He hoped the night would provide enough cover of darkness to keep the evacuation moving smoothly until they could cross the desert and slip into Mexico and the safety they sought there.

A distant scream broke the silence, then Osote appeared once again. "We have lost another scout, Tanaka Tom."

Before Tom could make a reply, another warrior appeared with an unlit lantern. He stood there, a silent volunteer, as Tom put fire to the wick. Then the youngster rushed forward to do his best to pick out a safe path.

"Hombre mío," Paloma called to him. "Would you not walk a ways with your woman and child?"

71

Tanaka Tom smiled at her. "It's a rather slow walk, isn't it?"

"We will reach the bottom safely, never fear," Paloma said. "The people believe in what you do. It makes me proud."

"It gives me shame," Tanaka Tom said. "Today we have lost fighting men when I led them into the ambush. Now more must die as we try to leave this place in the dark. It would be difficult enough in the light of day."

"Send the old ones forward, *hombre mío*," Paloma urged him. "That way they will not die as useless baggage."

"I will not!" Tanaka Tom Long Knife said angrily. "And I don't want to hear any more talk like that. This I have already told both Osote and Guerrero."

"They would be proud to give their lives," Paloma argued. "You have said that the Japanese warriors live by a code that states duty is weightier than a mountain while death is lighter than a feather."

"We do live by that code in *bushido*," Tanaka Tom admitted. "But it does not apply to old people. They have reached an honorable and venerable state that calls for deference and respectful regard."

"This *bushido* is hard to understand," Paloma said. "Though I think we Apaches live by it too."

"*Bushido* will require me to kill myself if I fail here," Tanaka Tom said. "But it never requires torment of the elderly."

"That is stupid," Paloma said bluntly. "If you fail here and kill yourself, then you will not be able to perform more successful or glorious deeds in the future."

"It is hard to explain," Tanaka Tom said, though he recalled studying the war between Japan and Korea when Japanese generals committed the ritual suicide of *seppuku* when they lost a battle. The Korean commanders, on the other hand, continued to live and learn from their defeats. He pushed the logic from his mind. He was a samurai and would live—or die—by the code of that warrior class.

Two more pathfinders fell to their deaths before a blossoming dawn found all the people assembled at the bottom of the mesa. They were exhausted and aching from the long night of negotiating the steep, narrow trail but there was no time to tarry. They had to reach the safety of Mexico as quickly as possible.

"Let's keep them moving," Tanaka Tom urged the warriors. "We can rest after we cross the border. Remember—"

He was interrupted by the sudden blaring of bugles. The samurai spun on his heel and looked out to see an overwhelming number of blue-clad cavalrymen charging down on them.

Chapter Eight

Tom instinctively drew his long sword at the same time he whipped the Colt .45 pistol from the holster that rode low on his left side. "Warriors to the front!" he shouted.

"No, *hombre mío*," Paloma said joining him with his Winchester .44. "All young people—men or women—must fight this day. I have told your precious old ones to usher the children to the safety of the rocks at the bottom of the trail. Even now our own Pumito is being tended to by Flora, your former friend Lagarto's grandmother."

"Then find cover where you can and start shooting at the soldiers," Tanaka Tom Long Knife urged her. "There is little more we can do in the way of battle tactics."

The people of fighting age situated themselves as best they could and poured a continuous stream of fire at the advancing cavalrymen. There were far too many soldiers and they only slowed a bit under the Apache bullets.

More bugle calls and shouted commands followed as the troopers dismounted and began finding positions within the various sized boulders that offered good cover. Then, after only a few minutes, they began utilizing the one superior thing they had in comparison to the savage Apaches— discipline.

Through fire and maneuver, MacNally's squads advanced toward Tanaka Tom and his friends. Their quick rushes provided only elusive, difficult targets. Only a few blue-clad bodies dotted the area as they slowly, undeniably closed the distance between themselves and the people of the Ancha Mesa who fought so desperately.

"Move back into a tighter group," Tanaka Tom ordered. "The more spread out we are, the easier they can mop us up a few at a time. We must become one fighting mass. Now hurry!"

Paloma stayed beside the samurai, instinctively knowing that he needed covering fire while he directed the battle. Several unfortunate soldiers were spun and dropped by the heavy .44 slugs as she protected her man with the deadly rage only a female can muster in times of danger.

"Look, *hombre mío!*" she shouted pointing skyward. Several undersized arrows flew through the air toward the enemy positions. "Even the small boys have joined the fight."

"We need all the help we can get," Tanaka Tom Long Knife acknowledged. By then the soldiers had begun volley firing as bullets, literally flying in a deadly metal hail, slammed into the Apache positions.

"It is only a matter of time, isn't it?" Paloma asked.

"It appears so," Tom said. He glanced around to note several more of the Indian people sprawled lifeless within the rocky fortress they tried so hard to defend.

A sudden, urgent bugle call broke above the sounds of the fighting. Immediately, hoarse cries erupted from the soldiers and they poured out of their cover and charged toward the Apaches.

Tanaka Tom and his friends did pitifully little in stemming the attack as the blue mass swarmed into their positions.

The Six-gun Samurai, knowing his pistol would be of little use, holstered it and brought the *katana* into the fight. A burly, red-haired soldier leaped from a boulder at him. Tom swung the sword out, then drew it down in a graceful sweep as he pivoted around. The horse soldier's head,

74

mouth still open in a battle cry, bounced over several rocks before rolling to a stop.

Another trooper, not taking time to load, charged with his carbine held as a club. He swung hard, but Tom leaped back in time and the blow only grazed his head leaving a long, but shallow gash. Instinctively he utilized a horizontal stroke that slashed through his assailant's belly, spilling guts and body fluids to the dirt. The soldier, horrified at the sight of his innards, only had to bear the sight for an instant before the next two cuts both decapitated him and split his body like a lightning-struck tree trunk.

Another trooper, enraged at the sight of his mutilated buddy, charged in from Tom's blind side. He pulled back the single-shot Springfield carbine in preparation for the death blow, but a split second before completing the attack he was blown back as a .44 bullet from Paloma's weapon slammed into his side. The man, a strong and husky old soldier, miraculously kept on his feet despite the massive wound. He staggered in a small circle, his face twisted in fury as he glared at the woman who had shot him.

"Stinkin' Apache bitch!" he hissed through clenched teeth.

The second slug lifted him off his feet and he collapsed to the sand in a bloody, cursing heap. Paloma, furious because he still lived, once more took aim. But Tanaka Tom Long Knife, stepping back from the fighting, put a restraining hand on her arm. "Do not shoot him again, *mujer mía*," he said. "He is strong and brave, but now too hurt to harm anyone. I do not think it is his *karma* to die today."

"I will not kill him, *hombre mío*," Paloma said. "But not because of pity . . . rather in obedience to my husband."

The battle continued as the troops pressed relentlessly on, compressing the battle into a tight confined space within the rocks at the base of Ancha Mesa. Finally a bugle call sounded several times and the soldiers, skillfully employing covering fire, withdrew and then ceased fighting altogether.

Osote, his shoulder bleeding from a superficial bullet

wound, joined Tanaka Tom at his position in the rocks. "The soldiers have quit fighting, Cuchillo Largo. Have we beaten them? It seems impossible."

"No," Tom said sadly. "They are far from beaten. In fact, it is ourselves who shall know defeat in only a short time. The soldiers are regrouping to concentrate their strength for one final attack. Their commander is skilled and knowledgeable, and he knows he has won."

"I shall tell everyone to sing their death songs," Osote said. "As for me, this is my last day on earth. Let us find Guerrero so the three of us can die together and find ourselves in front of Spirit Woman at the same time."

"But first send the women and children away," Tom urged him. "They cannot help us any more. It is better they be spared the bloodlust of the victorious soldiers. There will be a massacre."

"No! No!" Paloma screamed. "I will die with you too, *hombre mío!*"

"Go back and take care of our son," Tanaka Tom said. "I won't have his brains dashed out against a rock by some enraged soldier."

"You always speak of *karma*—fate," Paloma said. "If Pumito is murdered in such a manner, then it is already willed. That is by your own beliefs."

"Now I do not speak of *karma*," Tanaka Tom Long Knife said sternly. "I speak of obedience. Go take care of our son and hide on the rocks until the situation is under control and the troops have calmed down."

"No!" shouted Paloma. Her stone-age passions suddenly flared up out of control and the young Apache woman lost all of her sensibilities. She emitted a loud warcry, her eyes lit with savage battle lust.

Tanaka Tom, recognizing her growing hysteria, did what he thought best to bring her under control. He struck her so hard Paloma fell at his feet. "I told you what to do! *Now do it!*"

Both the slap and the authority in his voice calmed her, and although now weeping she was under enough emotional control to do what Tanaka Tom thought best. As she got to her feet and walked away, Osote and Guerrero joined the Six-gun Samurai. Guerrero, his swarthy face even darker from powder stains, showed his white teeth in a fierce grin. "Ayi-eee! It is a good day to die!"

"Good or not," Tanaka Tom said. "Today we shall indeed die."

The warriors, their death chants intermingling in tuneless melodies, prepared themselves for the final assault. Cartridges were laid out in convenient piles close by as cutting weapons were also put in handy spots to use after the last bullets had been fired.

The urgent staccato of *Charge* was sounded by a bugler over in the cavalry positions.

"Prepare yourselves!" Tanaka Tom shouted.

Deep throated shouts welled up from the blue ranks that swarmed over the covering rocks in front of them.

"Die bravely, like Ancha Mesa Apaches!" Osote yelled to the Indians.

The soldiers, well organized and disciplined, now combined their shooting and maneuvering as they pressed forward relentlessly against the weak volleys the Apaches were able to muster.

"Remember this, Warriors," Guerrero bellowed. "Our children watch us now. They will tell stories and sing songs of this, the final battle of the people of the Ancha Mesa, so give them glorious tales and legends to pass on."

The soldiers reached the final open position, then quickly formed up in their dense ranks and ran forward to bring the battle to its inevitable end.

A sudden firing from one side that staggered the troops' formation steadily increased in volume until the soldiers' attack began coming apart.

The Thunder Eagles, led by a screaming El Mesias, charged in from the flanks and literally rolled over the hapless soldiers. Officers and sergeants shouted frantic orders as the troops withdraw back to their original positions. Even this was not enough as the overwhelming assault of the Apache war society drove them even from there.

Within fifteen minutes the only cavalrymen left were the dead and wounded that littered the area. El Mesias, his face contorted into a triumphant sneer, rode up to Tanaka Tom Long Knife and looked down on him.

"Once you saved the Ancha Mesa people, Cuchillo Largo," the Indian said. "Now we have saved you. The debt is cancelled and no person of our clans owes you a thing. Therefore you are on your own as far as I am concerned, and if I ever see you again I will kill you . . . roast your body over a fire . . . and consume your flesh like an animal's. I have spoken, Cuchillo Largo!"

Then, without waiting for a reply, the maniacal young man wheeled his horse and led his howling band off into the desert.

Tanaka Tom looked toward the far desert horizon. Now, after two days of hard traveling, the bulk of the people had disappeared from his view into the blurry heat waves that danced above the ground. The Six-gun Samurai glanced to his rear at the slowly moving group he accompanied.

These were the old people. Gray-haired and wrinkled, these ancient Apaches were nearing the limit of their endurance. Bodies that once withstood hunger and thirst for days, that had been trained to operate on raw nerve long after near complete exhaustion had set in, now faltered as their younger tribesmen pressed on. Only the relentless Cuchillo Largo stuck with them.

One old man named Castor called out in a weak, hoarse voice. "Cuchillo Largo, I would speak with you."

The samurai, ever respectful of the aged, rode up and politely dismounted. "I am at your service, Castor-*San*."

"That is the trouble, Cuchillo Largo," the old man said. His leathery, incredibly wrinkled face showed a marked disapproval of the younger man. "You should not be at my service. Or anyone else who walks in this miserable, useless band."

Tom smiled. "My beliefs include reverence of old age."

"Bah!" Castor said undiplomatically. "Old age is but Spirit Woman's way of letting one know that death is near. Why else would she let a good body cripple up and ache? She is telling people to prepare to meet her. It is not a bad thing."

78

Tom thought a moment, trying to come up with some way to say what he felt in words the old Apache could relate to. Finally he said, "In the country of Japan it is believed that old age makes strong medicine. The minds of the ancients hold much wisdom and good advice."

Castor shook his head. "Our life is simple, Cuchillo Largo. By the time an Apache has reached his fifteenth year he already knows all things in our culture. He can fight in war, hunt, take a woman and survive . . . *survive!* That is what our ways are all about, Cuchillo Largo. And old weak people like myself and these others do nothing to insure the clan's survival. Therefore we no longer serve a purpose and must be left to die."

The samurai, who had grown angry with warriors for speaking the same thoughts, felt no irritation toward the bow-legged ancient who stood before him. "Castor, I must do what I think is right. Maybe you are a wiser man than I, but if I am a stupid man, at least I feel good about what I am doing."

Castor suddenly squatted down. "I shall go no farther. You are a fighting man. It would be a pity if you wasted your life on me."

"Or me!" an old squaw said. She imitated Castor. Soon all the old ones were on their haunches looking up at the Six-gun Samurai in impassive insolence. The old woman sneered "I would rather have died on the Ancha Mesa than here. It is much nicer than the desert, no?"

"If you come with me you may still die in your homeland," Tanaka Tom Long Knife said. "Our plan is difficult but not impossible."

Castor stood up and started to speak again, but the bullet struck his jaw blowing it spinning into the air to land in front of the old woman. He grasped at the bloody nothingness below his nose and fell writhing to the sand.

Tanaka Tom turned in his saddle in time for the *bandido* who had sneaked up with his comrades to leap on him. Both crashed to the ground. Tom rolled to his feet and lashed out instinctively. The edge of his boot caught the Mexican's throat in a *soku-to* kick smashing the windpipe into a bloody pulp. The samurai whirled on his heel and drove the edge of his hand across another's nose in a *shuto* blow, but two more simultaneously tackled him.

He fought to his knees as both held onto his arms in desperation. Tanaka Tom took a deep breath and just began the maneuver to throw his assailants from him when a pistol barrel crashed down on his head. Even as he lost consciousness, his blurring vision caught the sight of the old people he had sworn to protect being scalped as they writhed in silent pain, held in the grips of Chaparro's bandits.

* * *

Chaparro stepped out of his hut and walked to his chair on the crude veranda built out from the domicile. The moment he sat down, a group of his men, leading a prisoner, approached him respectfully.

"We are back from the raid, *Don* Chaparro," Tomas said. He threw down a bloody sack. "Scalps," he explained. "Eighteen all told. But they'll have to be dyed."

Chaparro nodded his understanding. "Old ones, eh? Where did you find them? Tied to some trees or bushes?"

"No, *Don* Chaparro," Tomas answered. He indicated Tanaka Tom with a sweep of his hand. "This big one here was guarding them . . . or at least taking care of the *viejos*."

Chaparro eyed Tom closely. "Bring him forward. What sort of man—a *gringo*—takes care of old Apaches?"

"We know this one," Tomas said hastily. "It was he who broke up our attack . . . you know, *Don* Chaparro, the one you had Martinez shot about."

"Ah! Then this was the *diablo* that scared Martinez."

"The same. Look! Here are his swords," Tomas said handing over the *katana* and *hotachi*.

Chaparro quickly eyed the two weapons. He drew the longer and checked the edge. "Sharp, no? But toys just the same." He watched carefully as the samurai was wrestled up to him. "Why do you fight with swords, *Gringo?*"

Tanaka Tom stood silent.

"I guess you don't like to talk," Chaparro said. "When

80

I first heard about you I thought you were something special. But I suppose not.''

"What shall we do with him, *Don* Chaparro?" Tomas asked.

"Shoot him," Chaparro answered offhand. "Anybody want these things?" He held out the swords but none of the *bandidos* expressed an interest in the weapons. The bandit leader tossed them aside, but spent several long moments closely inspecting Tom. "Maybe you're not a *gringo*. Are you a *gitano*—a Gypsy?"

The Six-gun Samurai again elected to remain silent.

Tomas slammed his fist into the small of Tom's back. "When *el jefe* asks you a question, you answer!"

Tom pivoted on his foot and drove a high *yoko geri kekomi* kick into the bandit's jaw. Tomas' *sombrero* flew off his head as its owner sank into unconsciousness. Another bandit leaped forward with knife drawn, but one more lightning-like kick, this time a *mae geri keage*, broke his wrist and the numbed hand was unable to hold onto the weapon. Tom turned again and found himself facing Chaparro's drawn pistol.

Chaparro grinned. "I admire a fighting man, but I guarantee I will shoot you before you manage one of those fancy kicks of yours in my direction, *Señor*. Now will you behave yourself?"

Tom knew this to be no time to test Chaparro's speed or reflexes. "Treat me with dignity then, and I shall conduct myself with decorum."

"That sounds reasonable," Chaparro said. "I am called Chaparro."

"I am Thomas Fletcher and I am an American," Tom said politely.

"Well," Chaparro said proudly. "I am *mexicano*, and the leader of this band of brave men. We are going to shoot you, *Don* Thomas Fletcher, but you have struck my fancy. Do you have any last requests?"

Tanaka Tom decided that if his life were to end at that point he would accept the fact graciously as *karma* should be. Then why not enjoy one of life's greatest pleasures as a final gesture. "I would like a woman."

Chaparro leaned his head back and laughed long and hard. "What an *hombre!* He faces a firing squad with a standing *verga!* The least we can do is provide a hot woman to cool his passions, no?"

"Let's get him one of the old hags," one bandit suggested.

"*¡Barboso!* Such bravery deserves better than that," Chaparro said. "Get him one of the recent captives . . . but one who has been broken in. Why should he have to work up a sweat by raping some young virgin, eh?" He turned to Tom. "Unless that is what you prefer."

"I think an experienced woman would be more pleasant," Tanaka Tom said.

Chaparro sent one of his personal bodyguards off, then turned his attention back to the samurai. "Tell me, *Don* Thomas, what were you doing with those miserable Apaches?"

"They were friends of mine," Tom said, being careful not to mention the rest of the group.

"And what were those old folks doing out by themselves like that?" Chaparro asked.

"They had been banned from their village," Tanaka Tom lied. "I felt pity for them and went on their journey to see if I could be of help to them."

Chaparro laughed and indicated the bloody bag of scalps. "It appears you didn't serve much purpose, eh?"

"I suppose not," Tom said. "But I didn't expect to be able to do much."

"Then you were a real *estúpido*," Chaparro said. He looked past the prisoner. "Ah! Here comes your prize."

A rather pretty, light-skinned Mexican girl was pushed forward. Obviously she had accepted the fact that she was completely at the mercy of her captors. She smiled somewhat feebly.

"This *gringo* wants a woman before we shoot him," Chaparro said. "You give him pleasure, eh?"

The girl's smile became more sincere when she noted the handsome stranger. "Of course, *Don* Chaparro. Whatever you say."

Chaparro started to make another remark when a messenger suddenly appeared. "*Rurales*, have arrived," the man said, out of breath from running. "With pesos for scalps."

"Good," Chaparro said happily. "Take this bag and dye that gray hair black *pronto*. I will talk with the commander of the *Rurales* while we wait."

Within moments *Capitan* Francisco Moreno strode up to the bandit chief. "We hear you have several Apache scalps to turn in for bounty."

Chaparro smiled. "Nice of you to take the trouble of bringing the money out to us."

Moreno remained solemn. "A few bribes you've placed in Nogales undoubtedly account for my receiving orders to accord you this special attention."

"No doubt," Chaparro said. "By the way, this *gringo* here was with the Apaches. He says he is their friend."

Moreno coldly eyed the samurai. "You ride with the Ancha Mesa *indios?*"

"I do," Tom answered.

Moreno turned back to the bandit leader. "Then I insist you turn him over to me to deliver to Mexican justice. If he rode with the raiders he legally belongs to me."

Chaparro smiled and shrugged. "Well, too bad for him, eh? I was going to let him have a woman before I shot him. But far be it from me to interfere with the law, *correcto?* In that case, I gladly release him to your custody as any good Mexican citizen would, *Capitán* Moreno."

Moreno returned the smile. "I am sure the *república* appreciates your good services, *Don* Chaparro."

Chaparro accepted the compliment with a slight nod of his head. "This strange *hombre* had swords with him, *Capitán*. Those of you who wear uniforms doubtlessly appreciate such useless baubles more than I, no? I'll have one of my men fetch them for you."

Moreno smiled. "Another legal gesture on your part, *Don* Chaparro. Since this man is now a prisoner of the

Mexican Republic, all his property now belongs to our benevolent government.''

Chaparro turned to Tanaka Tom. ''Sorry, *Gringo*, but my country calls on my patriotism, though actually I don't really give a damn who executes you . . . just as long as you are shot.''

Chapter Nine

Three days of napping and idleness broken only by an occasional meal of tortillas and beans finally came to an end for Tanaka Tom when he was taken from his cell at the *Rurale* garrison of Fortaleza Moreno. An escort of four guards marched him into the post's headquarters building.

Capitán Francisco Moreno, his countenance stern and angry, eyed his prisoner for several long moments before he spoke. ''So! You say your name is Thomas Fletcher, eh?''

''Yes,'' Tanaka Tom said.

''Mmmmph! And how am I supposed to believe that?'' The samurai shrugged. ''I don't know.''

Moreno stood up and tugged at his tunic. ''Well, if you don't know, then I certainly don't either . . . perhaps your name is . . .'' He paused dramatically then leaned forward. ''Jesse James, eh?''

''No,'' Tanaka Tom said.

''I think maybe there is a big reward for you up in the United States,'' Moreno said. ''You look like a desperate criminal who has committed many heineous crimes.''

''Then perhaps you should take me to the American authorities,'' Tanaka Tom said. ''Such an action would serve two purposes. I will be delivered to justice and you will get a lot of money.''

Moreno sat down. ''You do not fool me, I know you are

not Jesse James. But you have committed horrible crimes, have you not?"

"No," Tanaka Tom answered.

"Then why are you allied with a tribe of fiendish Apaches?"

"Your choice of adjectives is not only slanted, but puts me in a very difficult position when I try to tell you the truth," Tanaka Tom said.

"An honest man fears no questioning or probing," Moreno countered with a smirk.

"Really? Then may I ask you something?"

"Of course," Moreno said. "I am an officer of the law, and an example of decency and respectability."

"Fine," Tanaka Tom said. "Tell me, then, have you stopped beating your wife?"

"Yes . . . no! What, I'm not even married," Moreno said, reddening.

"Do you still take bribes?"

"No! I never took bribes," Moreno said.

"When didn't you take bribes?" Tanaka Tom inquired calmly.

"I always didn't take them ever," Moreno said. "That is . . . I never took them always . . . I have never . . . *espera*—wait!" He leaped to his feet. "I am the interrogator and you are the criminal! Conduct yourself accordingly."

"How many times in the course of a day's work do you break the law to suit your own purposes?" Tanaka Tom insisted.

"*Silencio*, or I will have you shot!" Moreno shouted.

"That is against even Mexican law," Tanaka Tom said. "There is a judicial procedure for you to follow."

"When I said I would have you shot, I didn't mean *I* would have you shot. I meant I would have others take care of having you shot. *That* is the Mexican way," Moreno said.

"Ah!" Tanaka Tom said. "Then you are indeed a forthright member of the community of lawmen. I congratulate you and am pleased to be in your august presence."

Moreno, soothed now, sat down once again. "That is

better, *Señor*. Now! Tell me of your involvement with the fien . . . er, the Apaches.''

''They were old, old people abandoned and left to perish in the desert,'' Tanaka Tom said.

''A common practice of many desert *indios*,'' Moreno said. ''But these were Ancha Mesa Apaches, no?''

''Yes,'' Tom answered. ''The bandits of Chaparro attacked and scalped them. Then they dyed the gray hair and sold the hideous things to you as if they were young people.''

Moreno seemed embarrassed. ''In truth they didn't exactly dye the scalps. They simply poured black ink over them.''

Tanaka Tom feigned anger. ''And you say you are decent and respectable!''

''But *I* am!'' Moreno insisted. ''However, my superiors in Nogales, alas, do not share my high morals . . . I am at their mercy.''

''And this is exactly what is happening to the Ancha Mesa Apaches,'' Tanaka Tom said. ''The peace loving ones among them are the victims of others who are evil and warlike. I have the honor of having been adopted into their tribe, and am fully cognizant of the situation. Because of one insane leader called El Mesias, the innocent are made to suffer. They have been forced to flee the comfort of their homes on the Ancha Mesa in Arizona to the Duro Mountains here in Mexico.''

''The Duro Mountains?'' Moreno asked. ''Good protection there, but not a paradise, *Señor*. It is a hard place to survive.''

''But they must stay there until the guilty ones are brought to justice,'' Tanaka Tom said. ''I am devoting myself to protecting these poor souls.''

''Commendable, *Señor*,'' Moreno said. ''I must tell you I abhor dealing with the blackguard Chaparro, but circumstances force me to. He is a powerful man and able to place money in the right places.''

''Sounds difficult for you,'' Tom said. ''But if you were able to bring El Mesias to justice, perhaps you could implicate Chaparro's crimes into the matter as well.''

86

"If my *Rurales* captured or destroyed the bad Apaches," Moreno mused, "then Chaparro could not get his hands on their scalps. Without money from scalping the *indios* he could not maintain his gifts of money to my *comandantes*, who in turn would then allow me to bring him to justice."

"Exactly!" Tanaka said. "Would you like to strike a bargain?"

"What sort?" Moreno asked.

"Let me tend to my end of this business, which will not only protect the innocent, but make it easier for you to defeat El Mesias," Tanaka Tom said. "All you must do is release me from custody."

"I must confess I believe in you," Moreno said. "The fact that you were with old people rather than warriors is proof enough of your innocence." The Mexican officer stood up and walked to a corner of the room where the samurai's swords had been placed against the wall. He returned with the deadly instruments and handed them over to their owner with a smile. "If you say that not all the Ancha Mesa Apaches are involved I know that is true. In my own poor way I wish to serve the law and protect the people, *Señor* Fletcher."

"I realize that, Captain," Tanaka Tom said sincerely. "And between the two of us we shall destroy both El Mesias and Chaparro."

Moreno shrugged philosophically. "Or vice versa."

* * *

The Apache warriors, the flames of several campfires casting shadows on their packed mass, stood before the awesome figure of El Mesias. Their leader was arrayed in his Thunder Eagle costume, the beak of the hat that represented the great war god's head, jutting out over his countenance. His eyes seemed to be as alit as he waited for his followers to settle into silence. Finally he spoke in the slow, deliberate tones with which he always began his addresses to them.

"Hear me, Thunder Eagles, for tomorrow the accomplishment of our sacred mission begins in earnest. Last night our great diety appeared to me in all his awesome

87

glory. The task he sets before us seems an impossible one, but he reminded me that what we do, we do *for* him and, more important, *with* him. And it is for the good and everlasting glory of our great Apache clans.''

A shout of approval erupted from the fanatical young warriors.

"First, Thunder Eagle wants me to tell you that when other races of men are destroyed, all Apaches, living or dead, will walk the land as the only people. Even the ancients who died more years ago than there are stars in the sky will return to the green earth to hunt once again. All warriors killed in this, our most sacred war, will also return. So do not sing death songs again! That is a command. Because death is forever ended for our people.''

Several warriors, overcome by emotion, fell to their knees and raised their hands high to praise the divine strength of Thunder Eagle.

"Therefore do not grieve or fear death of this great warrior society. Until the final day of glory, those Apache fighters shall make war as spirits under the direct leadership of Thunder Eagle. You must seek death in battle as a road to the greater victory of returning to the earth whole in body.''

A warrior, his eagerness overshadowed by more urgent drives, spoke out boldly, "What about our women, El Mesias? It has been some weeks and our loins ache for the comfort of our wives' bodies.''

"Thunder Eagle forbids you to couple with your own women in this war of wars,'' El Mesias cried. "If you wish to spend your passions in a woman's body, then it must be an enemy female. So you must fight hard and take them alive for your pleasure. Then when you have finished with them and your manhood hangs slack and limp, kill these bitches and cut them into pieces. Throw the hunks of flesh into fires and burn them so that no Apache seed is left alive in the alien bodies.''

The thoughts of such unbridled cruel sex brought howls of glee from the savage crowd of fighters.

"All male prisoners must be made to die slowly over our fires,'' El Mesias continued. "Their drawn-out agony

88

will release their strength for our souls to feed upon. Thus, through their pain we grow stronger and braver. Strip the skin from their bones in thin layers, plant them in the ground facing the hot desert sun with their eyelids cut off to let them grow gradually blind in the great burning light, sever their penises and stick them in their mouths to dishonor them, for all these things will please Thunder Eagle as they are done. He will reward us by hastening our victorious end to this war.''

Several warriors, already worked into a frenzy, began screaming unintelligibly as they struck out at others close to them. They were quickly subdued and, with foaming mouths and contorted faces, were tied up for their own and others' safety.

"You see?'' El Mesias shouted pointing to them. ''Already Thunder Eagle's spirit has entered some of you. Tomorrow morning we ride from here to end the contamination of this great earth by other men. They all must be destroyed! But there is one we must save to the last. For he is our greatest enemy and must suffer the most horrible death we can devise for him.''

One of the youthful fighters screamed in rage. ''Who is he? Tell us who he is so that we may be ready for him, great El Mesias!''

El Mesias raised his arms, his fists clenched tightly. ''He is a false Apache we have called Cuchillo Largo—but from this moment on he must be referred to by his White-Eye name: Thomas Fletcher!''

* * *

Cabo de Rurales Oscar Gomez urged his horse into the draw as he traveled slowly keeping both hands in sight. He glanced nervously from side to side as he continued on his way.

''¡Alto!'' The voice boomed out somewhere to the front.

Gomez reined in and immediately raised his hands over his head. ''Don't shoot, *por favor,* I wish to speak with *Don* Chaparro.''

The man who had shouted at him stepped from cover, holding a Winchester carbine at the ready. He gave Gomez a close look before speaking. "You are a *Rurale*, eh? Where is the rest of your detachment?"

"I am alone, *Señor*," Gomez said. "And I try to hide nothing. As you can see, I still wear my uniform."

"Dismount and approach slowly," the bandit guard commanded him. Another member of Chaparro's gang joined him and the two watched carefully as the *rurale* walked up to them. They quickly disarmed the soldier, then motioned him to move up the draw while they followed.

As the trio walked through the camp, the inhabitants looked on the *rurale* with undisguised hatred. They did not know whether he had been captured or deserted, and most didn't care. They would have gladly cut his throat simply for the good boots he wore. Gomez smiled and nodded with fear-filled eyes at the glares directed his way. *"Buenos días,"* he said politely. *"¿Como están?"*

The guards took him to Tomas who had been elevated to the rank of *teniente* as a reward for his good services to the gang's leader. He was eating at the time and looked up with irritation from his plate of beans and goat meat. "What's this?" he asked, indicating the *Rurale* corporal with a nod of his head.

"He says he wants to speak with *Don* Chaparro," the guard said.

Tomas quickly lapped up his food in loud gulps and smacks of his lips. Then he handed the plate to Sofia, the woman Martinez had given him just before his execution, and stood up. "What in *el inferno* does a lice-ridden *rurale* have to say to our exalted leader?"

Gomez, still smiling weakly, swallowed hard. "Please, *Señor*, I have some news for him."

"What news?" Tomas asked.

"I beg your pardon, *Señor*," Gomez said. "I prefer to speak personally with *Don* Chaparro."

Tomas lashed out with the back of his hand, the force of the blow causing Gomez to stumble back a few steps. The bandit followed this with a straight punch to the jaw that dropped the *rurale* to the ground at his feet. "Do not be so impertinent, you dog! I shall decide if you speak with *Don* Chaparro personally or not."

90

Gomez, who feared Tomas now, wiped at the blood on his mouth. His voice trembled but he felt he could press his position—especially with so many people now gathering around to witness. "I wish to speak with *Don* Chaparro on an important matter," he said loudly.

"You try my patience," Tomas said, drawing his pistol. "I think I shall blow out your damned brains for being a *rurale* bastard and the son of a whore to boot."

Gomez looked into the unwavering muzzle of the Colt. "What I must tell him is of the greatest importance," he said. "If you shoot me he will never know what intelligence I bring."

"What if I told you I didn't give a damn?" Tomas asked.

Gomez shuddered under the threat of instant death. "Then, I think when he finds out he will shoot *you!*"

A bandit in the growing crowd laughed aloud. "Go ahead, Tomas, either way we see some poor *bastardo* done in—him or you."

"Ah, *mierda*," Tomas swore backing down. "Can't you *estúpidos* see I am only playing with this *rurale* pig? Does no one here have a sense of humor, *por Dios?*"

"When do you want us to laugh, Tomas?" someone jeered.

Tomas swung toward the crowd. "Who said that? Step up and say it to my face!"

A tall, slim *bandido*, his hand dancing lightly over the butt of his holstered pistol, walked up to him. "I said it, Tomas, and do not play the tough *pistolero* with me, eh? You are a sneak knife-killer. I can draw and fire before you can put enough pressure on that trigger to shoot."

Tomas licked his dry lips, then laughed weakly. "Why should we kill each other, *amigo?* We both ride for our exalted *jefe*, no? I am going to drag this *hijo de la chingada* to *Don* Chaparro." He grasped Gomez by the collar and yanked him to his feet. After a hard kick to the buttocks, he shoved the corporal toward Chaparro's dwelling.

The bandit leader was sipping tequila when Gomez was pushed before him. Chaparro, quickly noting the uniform, was instantly interested. "*¿Qué está pasando?*"

91

"Some guards brought this *bastardo* into camp," Tomas said. "I decided to take him directly to you, *jefe mío*. He claims he has information, but I think the son of a bitch is just another whimpering *rurale*."

"Get the hell out of here, *idiota!*" Chaparro yelled at Tomas. Then he directed Gomez to a chair next to him. "Please, sit down, *Señor*, and forgive that *barboso*. He has no manners."

"He was very rude to me," Gomez complained.

"Oh, indeed?" Chaparro turned to a massive bodyguard who stood behind him. "Orlando, take Tomas over the hill there and beat him senseless."

Orlando smiled evilly. "*Con mucho gusto, Chief.*"

Tomas, who had already started to leave, began running as the larger *bandido* chased after him. Chaparro laughed aloud. "That will teach him to be polite to my guests, eh?"

"*Sí, Don* Chaparro," Gomez said delighted.

Only after drinks were served and a tray of *burritos* put out as snacks, did Chaparro settle down to business. "You say you have information for me, *Cabo?*"

"Yes, *Don* Chaparro," Gomez answered, wiping the grease from his chin. "I thought you might be interested in knowing that my commander *Capitán* Moreno has turned loose the prisoner you gave him the other day."

"Set him free? *Por que*—why?"

"They wish to form an alliance to make war on the Apache leader and, forgive me, you as well, *Don* Chaparro," Gomez said.

"Do you know this for a fact?"

"Yes, *Señor*," Gomez said. "I was in the room while they talked."

Chaparro nodded. "Then I must figure a way to get back at those two, eh?"

"Yes, *Don* Chaparro," Gomez said. "But I gleaned more information as well that might prove useful to you. It seems that *Señor* Fletcher has taken some of the Ancha Mesa Apaches, mostly women and children, to a stronghold in the Duro Mountains."

Chaparro was thoughtful for several minutes. "That is a bleak area, but easy to defend."

"A small party of skilled men can sneak in anywhere," Gomez said shyly.

"Of course," Chaparro agreed. "But why would I want a team of men to enter their village in those godforsaken mountains?"

"Because," Gomez said. "I learned that Fletcher has a woman there. She is an Apache called Paloma, and he is very fond of her."

Chaparro grinned. "You are a most intelligent man, *Cabo* Gomez. If some of my men managed to drag her out of there, I might bend this man Fletcher to my will and use him in several ways—or just kill him for escaping my wrath, eh?"

"*Seguro*—surely," Gomez said.

"My best sneak is Tomas," Chaparro said. Then he turned to another of his personal bodyguards. "Hurry over and stop Orlando from beating Tomas too bad, eh? I have a job for him. If I get my hands on this Paloma bitch, I could work it to my advantage. Perhaps this Fletcher will be heartbroken enough to deliver the rest of the Apaches to me."

Gomez smiled. "Fletcher and the woman have a son there too."

Chaparro laughed loudly. "Then we will sell his scalp as well."

Chapter Ten

MacNally threw up his hand as a signal for the long column of blue-clad cavalrymen to halt. His top NCO Sergeant Stensland rode forward and saluted. "Orders, Sir?"

"Dismount the men and have them walk the horses,

Sergeant,'' MacNally said. ''We don't want blown animals on our hands in case the need for hot pursuit suddenly arises.''

Second Lieutenant Richard Martin sighed with relief as he lifted his chafed buttocks off the saddle and swung to the ground. ''I never thought Shank's mare would seem so inviting, Sir.''

MacNally looked at his adjutant. ''Walking serves two purposes, Mister Martin. While it rests our mounts, it also adds to the men's physical condition. They tell me my grandfather in Ireland took a ten-mile walk every day of his life. And he lived to be in his nineties.''

''A wise old gentleman, Sir,'' Martin said. He looked around uneasily.

MacNally eyed him closely. ''You seem nervous, Mister Martin.''

''Well, not exactly, Sir,'' Martin said. ''But what we are doing would be considered . . . er, irregular in some circles.''

MacNally laughed aloud. ''Irregular, hell, Mister Martin! It's downright illegal. We have absolutely no right whatsoever to be here in the Mexican Republic.''

''Yes, Sir, I understand,'' the younger officer said. ''But if one considers we crossed the international border while in hot pursuit of Apaches, the conduct of this operation will pass the scrutiny of even the strictest of international lawyers.''

''We're not in *hot pursuit*, Mister Martin,'' MacNally said disdainfully. ''Hell's bells, there's not a goddamned Apache in sight, is there? As of this moment a courtmartial would nail my hide to the War Department building in Washington City. But when I get my hands on that son of a bitch Thomas Fletcher and wipe out his band of murdering Apaches, they'll pin a medal on my tunic front—and yours too, Mister Martin.''

''Yes, Sir,'' Martin said. ''You certainly have your heart set on bringing this Fletcher fellow in to justice. I just hope that—'' The young officer suddenly stopped talking in mid-speech.

"What were you going to say, Mister Martin?" MacNally asked.

"Er, Sir . . . I fervently pray that your *devotion to duty* doesn't . . . well, Sir, cloud your judgment."

MacNally's eyes narrowed in anger. "Do you think my conduct of this mission irrational, Mister Martin?"

"Oh, no, Sir! Not at all, Captain MacNally. . . ."

"There isn't a glimmering of an idea in the back of your mind about bringing charges against me, is there, Mister Martin?"

Martin swallowed hard. "Of course not, Sir!"

"There'd better not be," MacNally said threateningly. "I will not tolerate disloyalty for even an instant among my subordinates. Not officer nor NCO, Mister, so the concept of full cooperation had better be foremost in your mind."

"Oh, it is, Sir!" Martin said. "And always has been, Sir, believe me!"

"See that—" The sudden appearance of the scouting party interrupted him. "Hello! There seems to be something ahead."

They waited for the corporal in charge of the three-man detail to ride up and report in. The young trooper, his face already turning leathery from frontier soldiering, dismounted and saluted in one smooth motion. "Corporal Nadine reporting, Sir."

"Something ahead, Corporal?" MacNally asked. "Indians?"

"No, Sir," the corporal said. "Mexicans, Sir . . . soldiers, that is. Looks like a small detachment of twenty men or so."

"I see," MacNally said. "Fancy uniforms?"

"No, Sir," Nadine answered. "Plain looking, but they got insignia of a sort on 'em and the *sombreros* too."

"*Rurales*," MacNally remarked. He looked over at Martin. "A provincial police force of sorts."

"I understand, Sir," Martin said, glad that the subject had suddenly changed.

"Sergeant Stensland!" MacNally shouted. "Let's get mounted. There may be a confrontation brewing here."

Within a quarter-hour MacNally had his troops halted as he looked across a hundred yards of open ground to a force of *Rurales*. The Mexicans spent several long moments perusing the strangers before three horsemen rode out slowly toward them.

"Mister Martin, Sergeant Stensland," MacNally said. "Accompany me, if you please." He walked his horse forward while the others followed closely. Finally they came to a point some five yards from the *Rurales*. MacNally saluted. "Good afternoon. I am Captain Terrance MacNally, United States Cavalry, at your service."

"*Yo soy Capitán Francisco Moreno,*" the Mexican officer said coldly as he identified himself. He did not bother to add the polite *a sus órdenes*—at your service—as MacNally had done. "May I inquire as to your business in *la República de Mexico?*"

"Of course, Sir," MacNally said. "I am engaged in chasing a band of warring Apaches."

Moreno looked around, then shrugged. "Apaches? What Apaches? I see no Apaches!" his voice grew louder in anger. "There are no Apaches!"

MacNally knew he was on touchy ground. "Ah, yes, Captain. They are not in sight, but let me assure you that they are in the vicinity."

"In that case," Moreno said, "I shall take up the chase and capture these bad *indios*. I appreciate you informing me of their presence. There is no further need for you to remain here in Mexico."

"Perhaps if I continued the mission, Captain, it would prove beneficial to both my own great country and yours as well," MacNally offered.

"No, thank you, *Señor*," Moreno said coldly.

"I do have an advantage," MacNally said pointedly. "You have probably noticed that my own command is larger—much larger—than your own."

Moreno's face blanched in anger. "You are in my country in violation of international law and treaty, *Señor*. I must request you return to the border and cross it immediately.

"It won't take me long to defeat those Apaches,"

MacNally said stubbornly. "And I am also seeking a white man who rides with them as a leader."

Moreno's eyes lit up. "You are speaking of *Señor* Thomas Fletcher?"

MacNally eagerly leaned forward. "Yes! Do you know of his whereabouts?"

Moreno ignored the question. "If you pursue the Apaches led by *Señor* Fletcher, then you are after the wrong band. These are not the *indios* who are doing the raiding. The murderers are led by a madman named El Mesias."

MacNally was puzzled. "This El Mesias is leading Ancha Mesa Apaches, is he not?"

"He is, indeed, *Señor*," Moreno said.

"Then they are the same as Fletcher's group," MacNally said. "Both must be destroyed. And I know from personal experience that Thomas Fletcher is a murdering renegade and I am determined to see that he be hanged for his heinous crimes."

"What you are saying is ridiculous, *Señor*," Moreno said. "And your conduct is irredeemable and against the law. If you do not remove your troops from Mexican soil immediately you will suffer grave consequences."

MacNally laughed disdainfully. "As I mentioned before, Captain, my unit is larger than your own."

"This detachment is not the entire force of *rurales*," Moreno said. "There are many more—numerous enough to overwhelm you and your men. If you remain in Mexico, you do so at your peril, *Señor!*"

"We have spoken long enough. Good day, Sir," MacNally said. He pulled on the reins of his horse and galloped back to his men as Martin and Stensland followed.

"He has a point, Sir," Martin said as they halted in front of the men.

MacNally, his eyes blazing, turned on his subordinate, "If you interfere in any manner with the conduct of this mission, Mister Martin, I shall convene a drumhead court-martial and shoot you dead. Understood?"

Martin gulped. "Yes, Sir . . . you must want that Fletcher fellow quite badly, Captain."

"I want his ass so bad that I'm willing to risk a war

97

to get it,'' MacNally said. ''And, by God, I'll destroy that sword fighting son of a bitch if it's the last thing I do!''

* * *

Tomas lay in the sparse shade of the manzanita bush, his eyes watering from strain, as he watched the Apache camp. It had taken him and his four men all the previous night and most of the following morning to slowly ascend the eastern side of the Duro Mountains to reach their vantage point without being observed by the Apaches. His men, all personally handpicked, were farther down the barren hill, well concealed in a rocky outcrop.

Tomas' mission was an extremely dangerous one. He was to infiltrate the Indian village and quietly remove one particular inhabitant—the woman called Paloma. He had never seen her before, but he had been told she should be identifiable to him by her conduct as the woman of the band's leader as well as being in charge of the women and children. After several hours of painstaking observation, Tomas had finally picked her out. She had a baby, so in order to effect a quiet kidnaping, the child would either have to be left behind or killed. There was no way to properly determine the course of action to take at that particular time. The *bandido* only hoped that if the infant had to be left behind there would be an opportunity to remove its head in order to have the scalp to sell.

After all, a silver peso was a silver peso, *verdad?*

Tomas spent several long minutes studying the woman he had picked, then quietly crawled down the barren hillside to join his henchmen in the covering rocks.

''Did you spot her, Tomas?'' one asked.

''*Si*,'' he answered. ''She's wearing a scarlet calico dress. A sure sign she has some authority over the other squaws, eh?''

''*Seguro*,'' the other bandit agreed. ''She wouldn't wear a trading post garment like that to carry wood, eh?''

''I wouldn't think so,'' Tomas said. He shifted to a more comfortable position. ''Now listen to me, you *cabrónes*, I don't want anything to go wrong when we go

98

in to get that woman, *comprenden?* Her wickiup is almost in the dead center of the camp."

"*¡Ay, chingado!*" a bandit swore.

"I know it makes it more difficult, but not impossible," Tomas hissed. "Most of the men are gone . . . and that includes the *diablo* with the swords. They are probably out trying to hunt up some food. Frankly, those people look like they're about to begin a long period of hunger. They already seem tired and listless. That should work in our favor."

"*Dios,* in his mercy, smiles on us," another of the raiders said, almost reverently.

Tomas snorted a sarcastic laugh. "If God ever takes notice of us, he will strike our filthy hides with lightning. God is for *ricos,* not miserable bandits like us."

"Then let us pray to the devil," the bandit said, laughing.

"Just practice your naturally sneaky skills," Tomas said. "That's all you'll need to survive. We'll go in after midnight. Enrique and I will grab the woman. . . ." He gave the bandit named Enrique a threatening look. "And you grab her mouth, not her tits, eh? This is a kidnaping, not a rape."

Enrique grinned wickedly. "And after we get her out of there?"

"She belongs to Chaparro," Tomas said. "And I'm sure *el jefe* wants her delivered clean . . . without sperm dripping out of her *culo.*"

"Perhaps when he has finished with her then," Enrique said hopefully.

Tomas indicated two more of the bandits with a nod of his head. "Pedro and Javier, you two provide security. Keep a sharp lookout and prepare to lead us out of there, shooting if we're discovered."

The final bandit, a wiry little fellow named Roberto, looked up eagerly. "And what is my assignment, Tomas?"

"There is a child," Tomas said. "Kill it quickly and, if you have time, take the head. If not, drag the little bugger along with you. Just make sure he is dead and can't start squawking."

"I am too important to be a baby killer, *por Dios!*" Roberto said.

Tomas drew his pistol and shoved the muzzle under the other's nose. "*¿Qué?*"

Roberto gulped. "I will kill the baby, of course."

"Of course," Tomas said. "Now let's rest until time to move in, eh?" He settled himself onto the rocks to await the proper time.

The bandits let the hours slide by in silence, each lost in his own thoughts as they patiently awaited Tomas' orders to put the kidnaping into effect. They dully noted the ascending moon, looking from time to time to their team leader for some indication of activity until finally Tomas softly cleared his throat. "*¡Ya, vámonos!*"

They ascended the hillside slowly, each placing his booted feet down carefully as he walked. While there were no twigs or sticks to step on, many pebbles waited to be dislodged by some careless movement and sent clacking down the slope.

Tomas led them through the wickiups unerringly until they reached the one belonging to the woman in the scarlet dress. Pedro and Javier stood ready to begin shooting in case of discovery as the other three stole into the crude dwelling.

Paloma's double instincts as an Apache and a mother brought her immediately awake. She had time to grab the knife beside her bedroll and strike upward before Tomas and Enrique fell on her in a smothering, silencing embrace. Roberto, chosen to kill the baby, rolled over with Paloma's knife embedded deep in his throat as his life leaked away beside the infant he had been ordered to murder.

Tomas' grip on Paloma's throat cut off the flow of blood to her brain and, in only moments, she sank into unconsciousness. Without further thoughts for Roberto or the baby, Tomas and Enrique dragged her outside.

Javier, his carbine locked and loaded, took Tomas' signal and led the group out of the camp and back down the hillside where their horses waited.

Josefina Maria de Jesus Gonzalez-Martinez hid in the smoldering rubble of the little church, her hands clamped tightly over her ears to keep out the hideous sounds of screaming men who were being slowly skinned and burned to death by the Apaches who had invaded her village only a scant two hours previously.

Josefina's father had literally pushed and pulled the fifteen-year-old into the church at the first sign of the Indian attack. After shoving her behind the altar, he had gone outside to join the other men of their small farming village in their vain attempt to defend themselves. *Señor* Gonzales had been lucky. He had fallen early in the battle. His two sons were not so fortunate. They now added their own cries to the shrieks of tortured prisoners that died slowly at the hands of El Mesias and his Thunder Eagle warrior society.

The girl squatted with her head down, eyes squeezed shut so hard that tears flowed freely from them down her brown cheeks. Although her village had been visited by raiders before, they had been bandits who generally could be bought off for a few pesos. Or perhaps they would leave after playing a few rough games with the men (which might result in two or three injured, and only a rare death now and then) and raping several girls in a not always too cruel fashion as long as the women did not fight back and make it too much work. Then the bad men would ride on, the village would settle back into its normal routine to endure only bad weather, poverty, and harassing visits by *Rurales* or the Mexican army.

But Apaches were something else altogether, and Josefina hadn't been prepared for the horror the screaming savages unleashed on the small population of harmless *peónes*.

Suddenly she was seized by the hair and yanked upright. A howling Apache warrior pulled her by the luxurious black tresses from the altar and down the ruined aisle before shoving her through the door of the church. Josefina looked with terror at the scene from hell that met her gaze on the village square. Dismembered, mutilated and skinned bodies of nude men were spread across the area. Some lay still in death, while others writhed feebly in their final death throes. The torture was near completion by then, and the Apaches now turned their cruelty toward the women prisoners held off to one side. The warrior who now claimed Josefina as his own dragged her along to where the raping had already begun.

The first victim was Josefina's aunt. The screaming woman, arms pinned by one Indian while two more each held a leg as a fourth knelt between them thrusting his manhood into her body in a frenzy of hate and lust, endured the agony and humiliation as others were pulled out for the sport.

Josefina then screamed for the first time as her own clothes were ripped from her body. Naked and terrified, she tried to run but was tackled, the warrior slamming her into the hardpacked earth of the village square. He rolled her over and her fear gave way to frantic fury as she clawed at his face and hissed in her efforts to escape. But other Apaches quickly jumped into the picture and she was pinned to the ground, her legs spread open baring her virginal vagina to the mercy of the warrior's phallus.

His first thrust met resistance from her hymen, but his following actions forced entry as he bounced against her for long moments before spilling his seed inside her bleeding, torn body. Another took his place, then pulled away after ejaculating to make room for the next.

Josefina didn't know how many she endured, nor did she take notice of the ravishing of other women around her. And there was no time for recovery once the savage lusts had been satiated. Carbine butts smashed against feminine skulls spilling brains and blood, until the only living creatures in the small village were Apache warriors.

Then the buildings were set afire and all bodies thrown into the flames while El Mesias led his braves in howls of triumph and everlasting glory to the great war god Thunder Eagle.

Chapter Eleven

Tomas laughed wildly, then shoved the Apache woman down in front of Chaparro. Paloma hissed her anger and tried to regain her feet, but the bandit grabbed her by the hair and forced her to once again assume a kneeling position. "She is a wildcat, *Jefe*," Tomas said. "But we got her out of there just the same."

Chaparro looked down with open admiration at the savage beauty who stared up at him with such open hatred. "She has spirit and guts, eh? She must make love like a she-tiger in heat."

"All claws and teeth," Tomas agreed.

"You are sure this is the woman called Paloma?" Chaparro asked.

"Yes, *jefe mío,*" his subordinate replied. "I spent long hours observing the camp before I led my brave men inside. This spitfire was the center of attention, as would be the woman of a leader, and I heard her called by that name several times by others."

Chaparro nudged Paloma with his boot. "Your man is the one with the swords, *verdad?* Where is he now?"

Paloma made no reply; instead she let her glare of open hatred remain on the man who stood so insolently in front of her.

Tomas lashed out with his riding whip, hitting her so hard across the shoulders that it tore her dress. "When *el jefe* speaks to you, answer, you Apache *puta!*"

Paloma sprang to her feet so fast none of the *bandidos* could respond quickly enough. She produced a hidden knife from her blouse and slashed out viciously at Tomas. The Mexican recoiled in startled fear as the blade gashed deeply into his arm. "*¡Ay!*" he cried. Then he instinctively kicked out catching Paloma in the thigh. Before she

103

could retaliate with another attack, Chaparro leaped forward and pinned her arms to her sides. At the same time he pushed his loins forward against her buttocks.

"You are some woman!" he said happily. He grasped her wrist hard and twisted it, forcing her to drop her weapon. "I think a clever beauty like you should be searched." Paloma screamed and twisted as he dragged her into his shack. The bandits howled their glee and offered the gang leader encouraging comments and suggestions on how to tame the gorgeous prisoner in his grasp.

As he spun her through the door, he grasped at her skirt and pulled hard. The garment split revealing firm, smooth thighs. Chaparro's passions rose at the sight. Paloma tried to hold the ripped material closed as best she could. "My man will come and kill you, *Mexicano*. He will cut off your head and put it atop our wickiup for all to see and mock."

Chaparro smiled. "So the strange one with the blades is indeed your husband, eh? I am happy to learn that. A woman like you would be worth risking one's life for. So I am sure he will be coming after you."

"That will be the worst day of your life when he does," Paloma said.

Chaparro sneered sarcastically. "Then I must fill what short time I have left with whatever pleasure I can obtain, *verdad?* Will you fight me, or submit to my will without trouble?"

"No man shall place himself between my legs except Cuchillo Largo," Paloma said defiantly. "Only his thing and his seed enter my body, you filthy coyote!"

The bandit chief grinned at the sport ahead of him. "You offer much pleasure," he said as he once again grabbed her skirt. This time he ripped it clear of her body, revealing the beauty offered by the Indian woman. But before he could press his advantage, she leaped forward and bit him viciously on the nose. Chaparro screamed in pain as he beat at the persistent attacker who pressed her advantage until blood ran down the Mexican's face.

Chaparro finally managed to free himself and he gingerly felt at the damaged organ. The smile had faded from his face as he charged forward, the momentum of his attack bowling both himself and Paloma over to the floor. They rolled around the small, dirt-packed floor screaming and cursing as the Apache woman twisted her torso away not wanting even a fully clothed bandit between her legs.

"You will have to kill me first, *hijo de la chingada*," she screamed as she tried to force her fingernails into his eyes.

"Tomas! Orlando! *Ven aqui pronto*—come here quickly!" Chaparro hollered.

The two bandits rushed through the door and sensed the problem immediately. Without waiting for orders they jumped into the fray and, between the three struggling men, managed to subdue the woman.

"Hold her tightly," Chaparro said getting to his feet. "I do not want her beaten up too badly. We must put her on display so that anyone spying on our camp can easily spot her and see that she is in good shape. That will encourage the swordsman to attempt a rescue. But we will be ready for him."

Chaparro looked pointedly at Paloma who snarled her defiance despite being tightly held down. "And we will kill that *gringo* bastard in a way so slow that even Apaches will admire our skill. Then we will fuck this bitch until her guts fall through her *culo!*" He once again felt his injured nose. "Their deaths will be an event I shall remember with pleasure my whole life. *¡Ándale, muevense pronto!*"

* * *

Second Lieutenant Richard Martin took a shallow swallow from his canteen and made a bitter face. "My God!"

Captain MacNally licked his dry lips. "Almost better not to drink, eh, Mister Martin?"

"I went as long as I could, Sir," Martin said, "but I'd be willing to swear my thirst isn't slacked a bit."

"Your throat may feel raw and scratchy, but believe me when I tell you your body is making good use of even this awful water," MacNally said. "If it wasn't, you would have been dead days ago."

"Yes, Sir," Martin said sullenly.

"The water is sweeter the farther south we go," MacNally said.

"I sincerely pray it doesn't grow more bitter and alkaline," the younger officer said. "If we—"

A sudden outbreak of gunfire interrupted him.

MacNally stood in his stirrups for a better look forward. "By God! I hope we've finally run into those goddamned Apaches."

"We'll know soon enough, Sir," Martin said. "Here comes Sergeant Stensland with the scout party now."

A cloud of dust in the distance announced the approaching reconnoitering team as the men galloped back toward the main group. MacNally nearly trembled in impatience as the men approached. "Lord above! I pray you've finally taken me to that devil."

In less than ten minutes, Stensland reined up beside his commanding officer. He saluted sharply despite being out of breath. "Sir . . . a group of Mexicans . . . blundered into us. We exchanged shots."

"Casualties?" MacNally asked.

"None on either side, Sir," the sergeant replied. "When more of those pepper-bellies showed up, I ordered a withdrawal."

"Well done, Sergeant. Were they more of those wretched rural police?"

"No, Sir. They was bandits, Sir."

MacNally shrugged. "No problem there. If the miserable bastards bumped into us again, I shall order a full assault and litter this desert with their smelly bodies."

Stensland hesitated before he spoke. "Beggin' your pardon, Sir, they seemed well organized and led. I think—"

"When I want the opinion of a noncommissioned officer, I shall ask for it!" MacNally snapped. "Detail a new scouting detail and send them out."

Stensland's face was rigid with anger, but he saluted and kept his voice under control. "Yes, Sir."

A hundred yards away under the sparse covering offered by a thin desert bush, a young *bandido* studied the strange soldiers. He was puzzled by the uniforms they wore. He

106

had never seen that style before, but he made careful note of the peculiarities, knowing full well that Chaparro would be interested in these strange *militares* roaming the Sonoran desert.

* * *

The staccato of the drums lessened gradually until finally silence hung over the assembled warriors who sat in the dirt around the campfire. They murmured softly among themselves until El Mesias stepped from the darkness and stood in front of them. He followed his usual pattern of boring into his audience with a fixed glare for several long moments before he spoke.

"Thunder Eagle has spoken to me," he said quietly. "He heaps praise upon you for your bravery and fighting skills. The great war god tells me that the spirits of our brothers killed in the attack on the last Mexican village even now hover over us, waiting for the chance to take part in our next great victory."

A few spontaneous yells burst out from the young Apaches who stared spellbound at their strange leader.

"Now this Diety of Battle commands us to an even greater task than the slaughter of miserable Mexican farmers. He wants us to roll over and destroy the *Rurale* garrison the *mexicanos* call Fortaleza Moreno."

As El Mesias spoke, Lagarto squatted on his haunches in the back of the crowd. He had participated in every battle of their Sonoran campaign, but his original enthusiasm and exuberance had waned considerably as this warfare continued. Lagarto had been one of Tanaka Tom Long Knife's most trusted subordinates during the previous fighting with the U.S. Cavalry brought on by the crooked Indian Agent Bradford Cone. And, as such a trusted lieutenant, he had received a better-than-average military tactical training from the samurai. Now that martial education told him that the victories run by El Mesias were too costly in lives lost. True, this mystical leader said that the souls of the dead returned to fight alongside them, but Lagarto had seen little evidence of this. He had only noted with alarm the rapidly dwindling numbers of this band of warriors.

107

Lagarto was familiar with Fortaleza Moreno. He had been there several times, even inside on one occasion. The youthful warrior knew the strengths of the earthen fortress and the number and types of weapons used by the *rurales* stationed there. There was absolutely no doubt in his mind that an attack on such a strong position would result in horrendous losses at best and complete annihilation at worst.

He had no choice but to speak out.

He knew the danger of such an action. He swallowed hard several times, steeled himself, hesitated, then changed his mind as he finally stood up to boldly interrupt the mighty El Mesias.

"I would speak with my brothers!"

El Mesias' face twitched visibly at this unexpected act. "Who sounds his voice over mine and that of Thunder Eagle?"

"I, Lagarto," the young man said.

El Mesias trembled with rage. "Quiet! Only I am allowed to speak, and that is because I carry the words of Thunder Eagle."

But Lagarto persisted. "I do not like this idea of attacking Fortaleza Moreno. It is too strong for us."

El Mesias sneered. "You seek to give counsel to Thunder Eagle?"

Lagarto's face beaded in nervous perspiration. "I wish to dispense my wisdom in this matter to you, great El Mesias," he said respectfully.

"Wisdom?" El Mesias shouted. "Who are you to speak of wisdom? Thunder Eagle does not seek your advice, Lagarto."

"I know," Lagarto said. "But I hoped you would, Mesias. I have had special lessons in warfare given me only a short time ago."

El Mesias sneered. "For your sake, I recommend you continue to follow our path of glorious war without comment, young warrior."

Lagarto was insistent. "But it is folly to attack a position as strong as Fortaleza Moreno," he said, smiling uneasily. "The *rurales* are too many for us. Even when we make war on a small village we lose more men than we should.''

"Seize him!" El Mesias screamed. "And stake this infidel to the ground."

Before Lagarto could respond to the threat, numerous warriors charged him, knocking the Apache to the ground as they wrestled his weapons from his hands.

Under their leader's direction, the Indians quickly drove stakes deep into the ground and secured Lagarto's wrists and ankles to them as he struggled against the oppressive weight of dozens of his comrades.

"You will stay there until we return from our glorious victory at Fortaleza Moreno," El Mesias said, glaring down at the prisoner. "Then you will die a death fit only for a White-Eyes or Mexican to pay for your disrespect and insolence toward our mighty war god. Then, if the great Thunder Eagle is willing to accept your soul, you may once again fight at our side as a spirit warrior."

Lagarto, his hands and feet already growing numb from the tightness of his bonds, watched fearfully as El Mesias led the other warriors toward their ponies for the trip to Fortaleza Moreno.

Chapter Twelve

The shadow floated through the sparse desert vegetation in the darkness without a sound. It seemed without substance as it moved slowly, smoothly and silently toward the bandit camp. A dozing *bandido,* vainly trying to stay awake at his guard post, yawned in bored listlessness, unaware that the specter now stood behind him. No sound revealed the movement as the strange being stretched out holding a long, silvery object above its head.

Tanaka Tom's *katana* barely hissed as it traveled through empty air and sliced through the guard's neck. The head hit the sand with a dull plop while the body remained in a sitting position.

A scant eight hours previously, the Six-gun Samurai had returned to the Ancha Mesa Apache camp in the Duro Mountains to be given the awful news of Paloma's kidnaping. It hadn't taken the Indians long to read the signs left by Tomas and his cohorts. Mexicans—*bandidos*, in particular—had done the black deed, and Tanaka Tom Long Knife quickly reached the obvious conclusion of who was behind it. He had gone to his wickiup and immediately changed into the garb similar to that of the dreaded *ninja*—the masters of spying, assassination, and espionage of Japan—then the samurai spent an hour in deep meditation as he let his soul and body prepare for the deadly task of rescue he had decided upon.

Although he was without rest, the short period of inner concentration relaxed him, allowing strength to ebb into fatigued muscles as his mind was swept free of the cobwebs of exhaustion. When he was ready, he stepped from the wickiup, clad completely in black, a hood covering his head and face so that only his deadly almond-shaped eyes gave evidence there was a mortal man within the ghostly raiments of death. Even his Apache friends withdrew from him as he led his Morgan stallion through the camp, then quickly mounted and rode out into the desert.

Now he entered Chaparro's sleeping camp, hugging the dark of night around him like a cloak as he moved closer to the bandit chief's domicile. Sudden sounds caused him to stop and wait as motionless as a serpent until whatever or whoever it was either went on his way or proved to be no danger to him. Most of what he heard, however, were the snores of sleepers, some couple copulating with husky pants, or perhaps the futile weeping of some girl prisoner, tied up to be kept safe until once again her bandit captor decided to rape her.

Tanaka Tom knew he must be drawing close to Chaparro as the number of guard posts increased. Displaying patience and incredible skill, he began stalking these sentinels and eliminating them as he drew closer to his quarry.

The samurai eased up behind one heavily armed individual and suddenly clapped both hands simultaneously over the unfortunate's ears, causing a sudden concussion within the cranium from the abrupt vacuum the action created. Although it made some noise, it was minimal, and Tanaka Tom lowered his victim to the ground to avoid any increase in sound from the assault. The act was completed with a sudden *shuto* chop to the throat that smashed the life from the unconscious guard.

He started to move on when he was alerted by the voices of two men approaching him. He quickly dragged the dead man into the shadows and crouched to judge what new peril was coming toward him.

"*¡Ay!*" a voice exclaimed. "These long hours of guard duty are becoming a real *dolor en el cuello!*"

"Of course it's a pain in the neck," a second man agreed. "But how else is Chaparro going to get that bastard with the sword?"

"I don't know," First Voice said. "But I wish he would hurry up and try to get his woman. All these extra night hours are killing me."

"It shouldn't be long," Second Voice said. "Well, I'm home anyway. Have a good time looking after the woman, eh? I'll relieve you in the morning, unless the swordsman shows up tonight."

First Voice sighed. "*Muy bien*, I'll see you. The least Chaparro can do is let us have our way with her after we kill the *gringo*, eh? A fitting reward after so many stints at guard duty."

"You'd better hurry up to guard the woman or Chaparro is going to have his way with *you!*" Second Voice said, laughing.

Tom's heart beat faster in excitement and anticipation. The one man was obviously on his way to guard Paloma. Now he wouldn't have to waste valuable time trying to locate her. The samurai followed the disgruntled guard and was not surprised to note the man was walking away from the area most heavily guarded. Chaparro had intended to draw him into that part of the camp by concentrating a large number of men around a nonexistent prisoner. When the man he was following continued walking until he reached an outlying area of the crude village, Tom's hatred for the Mexican bandit chief didn't increase, but his respect did.

There was more talk as a short argument developed between the man being relieved and the one Tom was following. Evidently the new arrival was late and catching hell from his disgruntled friend. The Six-gun Samurai remained hidden until the angry *bandido* departed, then he moved in closer to check out the area being so carefully watched.

There was a crude but sturdy shack made of boards nailed to a frame of heavy timbers. There were no windows and but one door on which a large, iron padlock had been fastened. Every fiber of Tanaka Tom's being could sense Paloma's presence behind the lumber walls of the crude jailhouse.

The guard yawned noisily and crammed his hands deep into his pockets as he leaned against the shanty. The *bandido* evidently had every confidence in Chaparro's plans of throwing Tanaka Tom Fletcher off the scent by establishing a phony target to tempt him. The Six-gun Samurai was almost smiling as he moved forward, the *katana* unsheathed and ready.

A gentle swish heralded the blade's flight, the slight noise interrupted by the bandit's neck before Tom's follow through brought it once again into empty air. This time no head hit the ground; instead the cut had entered the neck and severed the spinal cord. Tom had to move fast to take care of the body. It had collapsed immediately, and the heels of the booted feet beat against the shack's walls. Tom pulled the dead thing away, then stood over it staring at the door that stood between himself and his woman.

He closed his eyes and began inhaling, drawing in the breath deeper with each repetition of the *zazen* breathing exercise. His mind focused itself like a channeled beam of light into his *hara*—that part of the abdomen which is the very center of man—until suddenly, like a silent explosion, his fist shot forward in a *seiken* punch driving itself through the door.

The wood splintered like a rifle shot, and as the crude

leather hinges sagged under the weight of the shattered portal, Tanaka Tom pulled it open and Paloma rushed into his arms.

"I knew you would come, *hombre mío,*" she whispered happily, as she buried her head into his shoulder.

The samurai had little time for embraces or rejoicing. Instead he took her hand and led her away from the scene of the rescue. "I had to make too much noise," he said.

"Don't worry about that," Paloma said, as she hurried along beside him. "These *cabrónes* drink themselves stupid every night. I have heard even gunfights erupt after midnight that did little to alert the guards."

"But they are waiting for me," Tanaka Tom cautioned her. "At least some of them are."

"But not close by," Paloma said. "Still, we should hurry."

The two skirted the fringes of the camp and slowed down to get through some chaparral. They had gone but a scant twenty yards when the chilling voice sounded at the same time the hooded lantern was opened on them.

"We have been waiting for you, swordsman," Chaparro said. "Do you remember me? I am the man who once condemned you to death, but our mutual friend *Capitán* Moreno embarrassed me by rescuing you. This was an act that spoiled my goal of having every man I sentenced to be shot executed without fail. But now I can keep my perfect record intact, no?"

Tanaka Tom said nothing as Chaparro's largest bodyguard Orlando stepped forward with pistol drawn. The samurai lashed out with a horizontal *ken tsui* blow from his left hand, which sent the Mexican's weapon spinning off into the night. At the same time he brought his foot down hard on the big man's instep. In only a milisecond he drove the heel of his hand into Orlando's chin and the lights went out for the bandit.

The second man jumped in instinctively and caught the edge of the samurai's hand across the bridge of his nose in a blow that smashed cartilage and bone into jelly. Then another upward punch drove the splintered mass back into the *bandido's* brains and he died without a whimper.

113

But Chaparro had made his move at the time of Tanaka Tom's second attack, and his punch caught the samurai on the ear. Tom hit the ground, blinking against the pain, but he rolled to his feet. Unfortunately, he received another onslaught from the bandit chief in the form of a well-placed kick dead on the chest. Tom went down again, this time gasping for breath.

Paloma leaped on Chaparro's back, forcing him to spin and punch at her as best he could. Finally, the Apache girl slipped and rolled in the dust as Chaparro cursed her in a guttural mixture of Yaqui and Spanish.

Despite his shortness of breath, Tom struggled to his feet and, using his elbow, slammed a *otoshi hiji ate* smash between Chaparro's shoulder blades. The bandit gasped and fell across the lantern, throwing the immediate area into total darkness.

"Cut off his head, *hombre mío!*" Paloma hissed.

Tom, growing dizzy from lack of oxygen and barely able to see, only grabbed her hand again and hurried her away as fast as he could.

Osote pushed his blankets aside and got to his feet. He had to stoop over due to the smallness of the crude wick-iup and he couldn't perform his morning stretch until he stood outside in the crisp dawn air. Then the Indian strode toward the high, natural wall of rocks that formed the fortress that the Ancha Mesa Apaches had used for generations in times of deep trouble.

"Osote!"

The Apache looked up, then waved at Guerrero who stood on the highest boulder. "What sights does the sun of dawn bring you, *amigo?*" he shouted as he hurried to begin the short climb to join his friend.

"A happy one," Osote's voice answered from the short distance. "Cuchillo Largo now approaches the base of our mountain, and his woman Paloma rides behind him."

"Are they well?" Osote asked, struggling up the rocks.

Osote waited the few minutes for the other to join him before he answered, "I don't know. I can only make out

114

our good friend's appearance from here. But he and Paloma seem to sit well on the big stallion."

Their voices aroused the camp and others, eager to see what transpired from Tom's rescue attempt, emerged sleepily from their lodges and scrambled unsteadily upward on sleep laden legs to get a better view.

The entire population waited the slow forty-five minutes it took Tanaka Tom Long Knife and Paloma to ascend the crude trail that led to the village. When the pair finally appeared through the opening in the rocks and rode into the camp, the Apaches showed their happiness with yelps of joy as they crowded around to touch the couple.

Paloma smiled and shouted out to the crowd. "Look everyone! My man, the brave Cuchillo Largo, has performed a brave and daring deed to rescue me. He has carried me back to my people and my baby. Honor him, for he is a great warrior!"

The cheering increased as Tanaka Tom reined up in front of his own wickiup. After Paloma slid to the ground and was swallowed up by a crowd of happy women, he swung down from the saddle, breathing uneasily. Chaparro's kick had been vicious and heavy, leaving a large bruise that stretched across both pectoral muscles.

Osote and Guerrero joined him, their presence causing the lower ranking warriors to step back respectfully.

"We must talk, Cuchillo Largo," Osote said.

"Yes," Guerrero said. "A time of decision has reached us."

"Very well," Tom said. "Let us go into my wickiup." He turned to Paloma. "My two friends and I would have coffee, *mujer mía.*"

Paloma, ignoring both the congratulations of her women friends and her own exhaustion, immediately rushed to prepare the hot, thick liquid as her man and his companions slipped through the door of the dwelling.

Tom settled down on his sleeping mat before speaking. "What matter are we to discuss?" he asked.

"Our food grows short now," Osote said. "And the hunting has been poor. It will not be long before real hunger arrives here in the Duro Mountains."

115

"And the springs are drying up," Guerrero added. "There is one so bad that its pool only fills up with enough water for one person to drink from twice daily."

"We must leave here soon," Osote said. "The limit of our stay is now drawing to its end."

"It will be difficult for us to leave soon," Tom said. "The *Rurales* may leave us alone for a while, but El Mesias and Chaparro are out there in strong numbers. We could never escape them."

"There is something else, Cuchillo Largo," Osote said. "Our scouts have reported that the pony soldier chief MacNally and many of his men are in Mexico now."

"He couldn't be!" Tom exclaimed. "He isn't allowed to cross the international border."

Guerrero shrugged. "Nevertheless, he is here, Cuchillo Largo, and he is but one more enemy searching for us."

Paloma entered the wickiup with large, earthen mugs of steaming coffee. "Would you eat?" she asked politely.

Both Osote and Guerrero looked to Tanaka Tom, but he shook his head. "No, we have too much to discuss now."

As Paloma left, the samurai's mind filled with the problems he now faced. Three, possibly four, strong groups of antagonists waited outside their sanctuary to attack him and his friends, and any group alone was large enough to wipe them out. At the same time, real suffering wasn't far away unless they could get out and find a more hospitable area.

It seemed to Tom that the Ancha Mesa Apaches had but two sure things in their future: slow death from deprivation or a faster one from annihilation.

Either way it added up to one thing: their complete and final destruction.

* * *

Captain Terrance MacNally watched as the bandy-legged little Mexican walked toward him in a rolling gait. White teeth gleamed in the swarthy face as he doffed his *sombrero* politely. *"Buenos días, Señor."*

The American army officer did little to conceal his disdain for the dusty little creature. "My scout says you wish to

116

speak with me. I do not speak Spanish, but there are a couple of my men who do.''

"Never mind, *Señor*," the Mexican said. "I can handle myself quite well in English.''

"Very well,'' MacNally said with a bored sigh. "What do you want to talk about?''

"All I wish to know is what *gringo* soldiers are doing in my country,'' the man said, still smiling. "I do not consider your presence particularly pleasing to me.''

MacNally snarled. "Who the hell do you think you're talking to, you greaser sonofabitch.''

"*Señor*,'' the Mexican said calmly. "I may be speaking to a dead man.'' He waved his *sombrero* over his head and suddenly dozens of armed bandits appeared on the crest of the ridge overlooking them. "My men,'' the Mexican said with a smile. "And I think it is obvious they outnumber yours by quite a few.''

MacNally was visibly shaken. "Just who the hell . . . er, would you identify yourself, please?''

"I am called Chaparro. And this land over which you have been riding so arrogantly is mine . . . *mine!*'' The façade of politeness disappeared as his voice became angry. "You answer my question, *gringo*, and you answer me now!''

MacNally swallowed hard. "Actually, well . . . I am in pursuit of a band of murdering Apaches . . . Sir. And the white renegade who leads them. He is a blackguard called Fletcher.''

"Fletcher!'' Chaparro exclaimed. "Thomas Fletcher?''

"Why, yes, you know of him?''

"At this moment I am leading my men in pursuit of that *hijo de la chingada!* He has killed several of my men in a most cowardly and un-Christian manner by cutting off their heads.''

"Then we are after the same goal, Sir,'' MacNally said with a weak smile. "Of course, I have the added burden of tracking down the Apaches too.''

"That is also my aim,'' Chaparro said. "Although I want the *indios* for a different reason. Their scalps are worth money to me.''

MacNally, who was well acquainted with the Mexican government's scalp-buying policies, nodded his understanding. "Perhaps, Sir, we might strike a bargain here. Even form a temporary but efficient partnership."

Chaparro thought a moment. "You might be correct, *Señor*. We have a lot of territory to cover, but between both our forces, we would be doubly effective."

"Of course," MacNally said, warming to the subject. "I have no objection if you take the scalps of the Ancha Mesa Apaches to sell. All I am interested in is seeing them destroyed and being able to truthfully report the matter to my superior officers."

"But I want that damned Fletcher," Chaparro said. "I will not turn him over to anyone else. I did that before and it proved of benefit to him."

MacNally shrugged. "If you wish to permanently eliminate Thomas Fletcher from this world, I certainly have no objection. Again, allow me to state that all I am interested in is the destruction of my country's enemies."

Chaparro smiled. "Let us take time for some coffee, *Señor*. We can refresh ourselves and work out the details of our arrangements."

MacNally offered his hand. "Of course, and thank you. Planning Fletcher's death will give me the greatest of pleasure."

Chapter Thirteen

Capitán Francisco Moreno rode uneasily through the Apaches as he followed his guide through the crude village. Finally they stopped in front of a wickiup. A beautiful Apache woman looked up at the mounted Mexican with open contempt. She turned her head toward the dwelling and said, "*Hombre mío,* you have a visitor."

Tanaka Tom Fletcher eased through the small opening

118

and stood up. "Hello, Captain Moreno," he said, offering his hand. "Please step down. Would you care for some refreshments?"

Moreno smiled as he slid from the saddle. "Yes, thank you, some coffee would be nice."

The samurai, who preferred tea but kept the other drink for his friends, nodded to Paloma who got up to fetch the pot from the coals. Tanaka Tom motioned to the blankets spread out in front of the lodge. "Make yourself comfortable, Captain. I apologize for the lack of good furniture, but we were forced to leave our main village and hadn't the time or facilities to bring luxuries."

Moreno smiled broadly. "Do not apologize, *Señor* Fletcher. I spend most of my time with my *nalgas* in the dirt. At least you provide a blanket."

Tom, knowing the customs of the Mexicans, did not press Moreno for the purpose of his visit as the *rurale* officer slowly savored the hot brew Paloma had served him. They made small talk until Moreno finally handed his cup back to Paloma with an indication his thirst was satiated.

"We are pleased to have you visit us," Tanaka Tom said.

"I wish I were here for pleasure," Moreno replied. "But I fear I have bad news."

"I appreciate you taking the trouble to bring it to us," Tom said. "No matter how distressing it may be."

"There are American soldiers over here in Mexico, looking for you and your friends," Moreno said. "They appear to be of battalion strength or a little less. Enough to destroy your band if they catch you in the open." Moreno glanced around the camp. "But I think you are safe here. Not even a great number of men could penetrate your defenses in such a spot as this."

"Unfortunately, we are approaching starvation and thirst," Tanaka Tom said. "We cannot stay here much longer."

"That is terrible," Moreno said shocked. "If you go out into the desert, everyone of you will die . . . believe me!"

119

"You're right," the Six-gun Samurai said. "But my previous training taught me how to handle such situations."

Moreno smiled. "Then you will succeed. I have faith in you, *amigo*."

"Unfortunately, the only path left open to us is extremely dangerous and nearly hopeless . . . but it offers us a chance, a terribly slim one, yet still a wild hope to escape."

"If that is all that's left to you, then you must do it," Moreno said. "If you die, you can die proudly, knowing you've done your best."

Tanaka Tom didn't bother to explain *karma* or its acceptance to the Mexican. "Our only salvation is the destruction of our enemies. And we have two . . . no, three, now. El Mesias, Chaparro, and a battalion of American soldiers."

"You make it sound simple," Moreno said. "Who are you going to get to remove your enemies?"

"There is no one," Tanaka Tom admitted. "Except ourselves. We must leave this place to attack and defeat our adversaries."

"You are horribly outnumbered," Moreno said. "I hesitated to tell you before, but now I must. When I reported the presence of American troops in Mexico to my superiors, they were only mildly irritated. That means I cannot use my men to help you against them. Nor against Chaparro, for he has bribed the authorities in Nogales. Perhaps I can keep El Mesias off balance long enough for you to handle the others. But it all seems impossible."

"It does, doesn't it?" Tanaka Tom said. "Would you care for another coffee, Captain?"

"No, thank you, after talking of your situation I would prefer a tequila," Moreno said grimly. "I feel as if I'm in the presence of death. Such an emotional experience calls for strong drink."

* * *

The *rurale* sentry gazed over the earthen parapet with sleepy eyes. Since *Capitán* Moreno had taken most of the garrison with him on the trip to Nogales, the routine of the post had settled into a lethargic schedule of undermanned guard duty, under the disinterested supervision of *Sargento* Romero, who spent most of his time sleeping under the influence of great quantities of mezcal.

The moon was but a pale reflection in the dawn sky as the eastern horizon reddened with the rising sun. The guard yawned, his mouth opening wide and exactly in time to receive the lance thrust that drove the bladed weapon through his throat and out the back of his neck. He gurgled in agony and grasped at the killing instrument that slowly drained away his life's blood through torn tissue and flesh. The Apache who had struck the blow howled his triumph as a signal to his comrades.

El Mesias echoed the battle cry as he motioned his men forward with a brandish of his medicine stick. The band of Ancha Mesa Apaches swarmed over the barriers to Fortaleza Moreno and raced across the small parade ground toward the barracks. Without hesitation they entered the adobe buildings and fell on the sleeping *rurales* who had little time to realize what was happening.

A young Mexican rolled from his bunk to make an attempt at the rifle rack in the center of the room. His efforts earned him two simultaneous bullet wounds that rolled him across the floor into the next row of cots. A screaming warrior leaped forward and drove his tomahawk deep into the man's face, leaving a wide deep wound that folded the Mexican's features into a hideous distorted grin.

Others died in the frenzy of hand-to-hand attacks as the butchery continued unabated for ten full minutes. When the carnage ended, the squad room was littered with over-turned bunks and the hacked-up bodies of *rurales* whose blood formed a widening pool that covered most of the floor. Two trembling, sobbing survivors were pulled from under the mass of corpses to be cuffed and pummeled outside where El Mesias waited. The prisoners were thrown at his feet as the Apache leader waved at the buildings. "Burn them!" he commanded.

The wooden roofs were quickly fired and the flames spread down through the lumber frames of the buildings until each was wrapped in a fiery wreath. Then El Mesias tapped the two Mexicans with his medicine stick and pointed to the nearest burning barracks.

"Throw them in!"

Eager hands snatched at the unfortunates and hurled them into the flames. The two leaped out, instantly beating at their burning clothes. Once more they were pushed into the fire, this time emerging with their hair burning as they screamed in pain. Again the two were forced into the burning building but they emerged slower this time, badly burned with blistered and charred patches of skin showing on naked bodies. Finally the howling warriors hurled them into the fire for the fourth time.

The two *rurales* did not reappear.

A sudden feeling of elation rushed through El Mesias' body at what he considered a great victory. He failed to realize that he had vanquished a weak and understrengthed garrison, and at that moment he felt he had eliminated the *rurale* threat from his area of operation.

"Listen to me, warriors!" he cried. "Thunder Eagle has given us a magnificent triumph this day! We have destroyed one group of our enemies and now we must continue to follow this sacred warpath until all other men who stain the purity of our land by living on it have been killed or driven off!"

The blood-maddened braves screamed their fanatical joy, leaping around their grinning leader. El Mesias waited until they had calmed down before he spoke again. "Now let us return to our camp. I have special plans for the infidel Lagarto." Without hesitating he turned and hurried out of the destroyed garrison toward the horses as his men followed at his heels in gleeful anticipation of Lagarto's fate.

* * *

Tanaka Tom Fletcher reclined on the blankets in his wickiup, his eyes closed as he let his inner-self drift into that special state between consciousness and unconsciousness that melts away fatigue and pain with a balmy nothingness. This art of relaxation had been an integral part of

122

his samurai training in which gentler sides of life were injected into the violent and deadly trade of war.

"Cuchillo Largo!"

The voice penetrated his reverie and he was instantly alert. "Yes?"

"It is I, Brujito, the son of Brujo. I would speak with you, Cuchillo Largo."

The samurai, wondering what the new medicine man might want, rolled from the blankets and exited the small dwelling in one smooth movement. "What can I do for you, Brujito?"

The Apache, who had taken his father's place as shaman after the elder's brutal murder, peered straight into Tanaka Tom's eyes. "My father set you on the path of becoming an Apache, but you have not yet reached the end of that journey."

"I thought I had taken part in all the ceremony necessary," Tom said.

"There is yet a small but very important thing we must do," Brujito said. "We must find your secret name."

"I thought my Apache name had already been given me," Tom said. "Am I not called Cuchillo Largo?"

"Indeed! Only that is not your *secret* name," Brujito explained. "That is a name that only you and I, along with the Apache gods, will know."

Tanaka Tom Long Knife nodded his understanding. "Then what must I do to learn this *nombre secreto?*"

"There is a special purification ceremony that takes place in the sweat lodge," Brujito said. "You and I will enter together and go into a trance. Spirit Woman will appear at the right time and tell me how you are to be called. I will whisper it into your ear after we emerge from the heat. Then never again will either of us utter it aloud."

"You mean each Ancha Mesa Apache has a secret name that only he knows?" Tom asked.

"Yes, Cuchillo Largo," Brujito answered. "When my father was killed he took many names to Spirit Woman with him. Even I, who served as his apprentice, did not know them. Only he and the other warriors knew this sacred thing."

123

"Osote and Guerrero also have secret names?" Tom asked.

"Every Ancha Mesa Apache warrior does," Brujito answered. "Even the treacherous El Mesias went through the ceremony when he first returned to our people—may Spirit Woman curse that day!"

Tanaka Tom Long Knife relented. "Then I too wish to have that honor. When is the ceremony?"

"Now," Brujito answered. "The lodge is already prepared. Let us go, Cuchillo Largo."

Paloma, who had been grinding a sparse pile of corn, spoke up excitedly. "Yes, *hombre mío*, you must go now. It is our custom. And it is a thing so sacred that I, a woman, was not allowed to speak of it to you."

"Then we should tend to this matter immediately," Tanaka Tom said.

Brujito, even now mentally preparing himself for the solemn task ahead, motioned for Tom to follow him. The medicine man led the samurai through the village as the people watched in silence at this commencement of one of their most sacred ceremonies. They walked past the camp's limits and down into a draw where an extremely small wickiup had been erected. Two warriors, dressed and painted for war, stood beside the compact structure. One stepped forward and held his war lance high.

"*Saludos*, Brujito! *Saludos*, Cuchillo Largo! The sweat lodge is prepared. We have danced here all night and sung the sacred songs of the ancients. All bad spirits have been driven away. This place is pure."

Brujito immediately began stripping and Tom did likewise until both men stood naked in the clear mountain air. As they stood there, the warrior who had spoken to them stepped forward and daubed warpaint on their faces. The design was a yellow lightning bolt on each cheek—the symbol of Thunder Eagle. Then the second warrior painted a wavy blue line across their foreheads—the symbol of Spirit Woman.

Brujito took a deep breath, then knelt down and crawled into the small opening of the lodge. Tanaka Tom Long Knife followed and found himself inside a close area

124

dominated by a pile of heated rocks. The samurai didn't appreciate the temperature inside until the arid heat began building up to a nearly unbearable intensity.

Brujito remained silent for a long moment until he finally began a sing-song chant as the temperature increased slowly but steadily in the small, confined space. Then Tom immediately felt a strange comfort as both his mental and physical faculties adapted themselves to the dry burning atmosphere.

For over an hour Brujito continued his chanting as Tom listened. Finally the interior seemed to be overwhelmed by a strange, white shadow that was so thick the medicine man seemed but a mere blur. More time passed and even Brujito seemed to slowly dissolve until he was gone.

Tanaka Tom now felt as if he were in another universe made up of a white nothingness. He sensed peacefulness and was at ease while he allowed himself to relax farther and farther into whatever mental condition he was attaining.

"Tanaka!" The voice erupted from the nothingness.

"Hai?" Tom answered respectfully.

"Tanaka Ichimara Tomi," the voice said, this time speaking his proper Japanese name in full.

Suddenly a portly, middle-aged Japanese appeared through the swirling fog. He wore a magnificent gold-embroidered silk *kimono*, both a *katana* and the shorter *hotachi* shoved through the *obi*. Tom, sensing a superior, immediately stood up then became confused. He had entered an extremely small wickiup yet he had managed to stand erect in it. He pondered the problem for only a quick second, then he bowed politely. "To whom do I have the honor of addressing?" he asked.

The man knelt down. "I am Soko Yamaga."

Tom's mind reeled in perplexity. Soko Yamaga had lived in the years 1622 to 1685. During that relatively short life, Soko, a brilliant intellectual leader and warrior, had been the one who originated *Bushido*—Way of the Warrior—the code by which the samurai lived, fought and died. Even a mentally and emotionally strong man like Tanaka Tom was staggered by this strange occurrence. He

125

stuttered like a young boy during his first *kenjutsu* lesson. "You . . . you are Yamaga-*sama*?" Then he fell to his knees and placed his forehead on the ground. "I am honored."

Soko accepted the compliment with a slight nod of his head. "You are well known to me Tomi-*san*."

"*I* am known to *you*, Great Sir?" Tom asked. "You are the man who taught the leader of the forty-seven ronin. Their revenge of their master's treacherous death honors him, and you doubly."

"Yes," Soko said. "After their *daimyo* was forced to commit *seppuku* for drawing his sword in the presence of the *shogun*, his forty-seven men played the roles of drunkards and louts until the opportunity presented itself for them to fall upon the enemies of their dead lord. They killed them, then went to the tomb of their master and all forty-seven performed *seppuku*. Such a magnificent and glorious occurrence is something for all samurai to hold sacred."

"Excuse me, Yamaga-*sama*, but why do you visit me here? I am only a humble warrior on a mission of vengeance concerning my family."

"Yes, you are humble, Tomi-*san*," Soko said. "But you are also a magnificent samurai and I have decided to take this opportunity while you are in this supernatural state of mind to visit with you during this brief period."

"I am listening, Great Sir," Tanaka Tom said.

"Your mission of vengeance is a just one," Soko said. "And I wish to encourage you to continue it. But I urge you to take time out like you are here with these people and use your fighting skills to help the oppressed and unfortunate. The Ancha Mesa Apaches are barbarians, but they deserve better than what they are getting. Compared to the Japanese and our culture, they are but a simple folk, yet they have honor and charm. I am pleased you have chosen to help them . . . even die with them if necessary."

"Yes, Yamaga-*sama*," Tom said.

"Please remember my basic philosophies," Soko said. "The samurai must do more than live off other people. He

126

must make himself a model of behavior, virtue and leadership. Others must look up to him and respect him."

"I understand, thank you," Tanaka Tom said.

"You must hold a moral superiority, for in that is great strength," Soko said. "And do not neglect the arts, Tomi-san. There is also nourishment in the gentle and the beautiful."

"Yes, Honored Sir,"

Soko got to his feet. "I go now. Perhaps we can have this opportunity to speak again, Tanaka Ichimara Tomi. Your deeds and conquests have attracted much attention from those of us who approach *nirvana*—the perfect state. Do not falter in your convictions or your beliefs. Conduct everything you must do according to *Bushido*."

"I shall do that," Tanaka Tom said.

"*Sayonara*, Tomi-san," Soko said. Then he stepped back and was swallowed up by the brilliant shadows.

"*Sayonara*," Tom said. He started to get to his feet when he felt hands tugging at him.

Within seconds he was standing outside the sweat lodge beside Brujito. The two painted warriors checked them over carefully, then walked away leaving the pair alone.

Brujito took several deep breaths. "I have been told your secret name."

"What is it?" Tanaka Tom asked.

"It is strange, because I do not understand what it is," Brujito said puzzled. "The sound is distinct but makes no sense to me."

"What was spoken in your ear?" Tanaka Tom said.

"Inazuma," Brujito whispered.

The Six-gun Samurai looked at the Apache shaman incredulously. How would a native American like Brujito know that word?

In Japanese it meant *Lightning Bolt*.

Chapter Fourteen

Paloma stirred the pot of *frijoles* simmering over the fire in front of the wickiup. These Mexican beans had been carefully and rigorously issued out to the families trying to exist under the harsh conditions in the Duro Mountains. With all the game now gone from the area, this was their only source of badly needed protein.

"Paloma!"

She looked up to see a dozen of the women approaching her. They were of various ages, from hardy squaws in their twenties to teen-aged brides with young papooses on their backs. Striding ahead of the group was one particularly aggressive gossip named Venida. Unusually tall for an Apache, her square face generally was unsmiling and solemn. Many a night the other villages had heard her berating her husband until her shrill, nagging voice evolved into shrieks as the man lost his patience and beat her.

She stopped immediately in front of Paloma and stood there, legs astride with her hands on her hips.

Paloma, who didn't like the woman, looked up. "Yes?"

"Our children are hungry," Venida said.

"So is my son," Paloma said.

"We are hungry too," Venida added.

"Then complain to your *hombre*," Paloma replied testily. "I am not the hunter for your wickiup."

"But it is you who passes out the food rations to us," the other said sullenly.

"I can only give you what there is," Paloma said. "There is not much. It is not my fault."

"Mmmph! You seem to have a lot of beans there."

"These are from yesterday's issue. We did not eat them then," Paloma explained patiently.

"*¡Qué extrana!* In *my* family, we were so hungry we ate them as quickly as we could," Venida said.

Paloma shrugged. "So? That is the Apache way. When there is food and drink, one gobbles them down before it goes bad or is stolen. But my man has a strange control over his body. He can will himself not to be hungry, thus he goes long days fasting. It seems to make him feel better and that leaves more to eat for a longer time."

"I don't think so," Venida said viciously. "I think you steal extra food for yourself from the stocks."

Paloma stood up, her black eyes snapping with fury. "You are a liar and an *estúpida!*"

Venida's face paled under the insult and she reached out grasping Paloma's long hair. The other responded in kind as each tugged at the other's lengthy locks. The other women, immediately taking sides, screamed encouragement. The fight developed from tugging and shoving to scratching. Within a minute both Paloma and Venida rolled on the ground, a pummeling, shrieking twosome. Clouds of dust rose up as the spectators followed the floundering, twisting fight.

"Enough!" Osote's voice broke through even the noise of the yelling crowd. This produced no results, so he and Guerrero had to wade in and physically separate the snarling combatants. Tanaka Tom Long Knife joined them. "What is the trouble?"

Paloma, speaking through heavy breathing, pointed at Venida. "She . . . said I . . . was stealing . . . food from . . . the rations."

White anger swelled up in Tom from such an insult, but he took the harsh, primitive conditions under which they lived into consideration before he replied directly to Venida. "No one is stealing food. We all get an equal share depending on the number of persons in each wickiup."

Venida, knowing in her heart that he spoke the truth, hung her head. "Times are hard here. We must leave."

"Stupid woman!" Osote barked. "We men know that. Don't you think we are trying to ease our conditions and figure a way out?"

"I don't know," Venida said sullenly.

"Go back to your wickiup," Osote commanded her. Then he waved the others off. "All of you! Return to your lodges and tend to your business."

As the women moved away, Tom took Paloma's arm and gently led her back to the cookfire. "She did not hurt you?"

"Of course not!" Paloma said disdainfully. Then she changed the subject. "Are you hungry?"

"No," Tom answered.

"You must be, *hombre mío*. You did not eat yesterday, nor the day before."

"I kept back some rice," Tanaka Tom said. "I nibble on it occasionally when I feel the need. That means there is less need for food at our lodge, thus someone else might eat a bit more."

"They do not appreciate it," Paloma said. "I fear that another enemy will spring up against us, *hombre mío*. This unceasing hunger will drive us against each other unless something is done."

Tanaka Tom Long Knife didn't answer as he sat down. He knew her words rang with the truth, and he had grown extremely worried about the situation they were in . . . at that point he had to admit fully to himself that their destruction was only a matter of time.

* * *

Lagarto's mouth felt like it was stuffed with cotton. The two warriors left to guard him acted as if the prisoner didn't exist as they took their turns at watch and ate and drank their fill from the war party's foodstocks. And Lagarto, raised in strict Apache fashion, was too proud to beg for relief.

He was into his third day without water when El Mesias led his triumphant band back into camp. Lagarto raised his head and, despite his exhausted and cramped condition from being staked out, had enough mental alertness to determine that few, if any, warriors had been killed in the raid in which he had predicted calamity. Perhaps, his

130

clouded mind told him, El Mesias had relented and called the dangerous undertaking off.

The young warrior could hear moccasined feet striding toward him. Suddenly the voice of El Mesias, calm and steady, broke into his reverie. "We have returned, Lagarto."

"I heard you," Lagarto replied wearily. He tried to relax in his bonds to show no strain. "What happened?"

"Why exactly what we planned," El Mesias answered. "We attacked and destroyed the *rurales'* garrison called Fortaleza Moreno. Every man there has been killed and the place burned to the ground."

The news was so stunning that it cleared Lagarto's head. Now his eyes took in the trophies of war displayed by the warriors. Some wore *rurale* uniform jackets or *sombreros,* while others sported other accoutrements of the Mexican police organization.

Lagarto licked his lips. "You have scored a great victory, mighty El Mesias."

"It is not *my* victory," El Mesias said. "Thunder Eagle and the ghost warriors fought for us. And you, infidel, said we couldn't do it."

"I was wrong to have doubted our god," Lagarto said sorrowfully. "And I am ready to accept the penalty."

"The penalty is death!" El Mesias cried as the others gathered around him. "You turned against Thunder Eagle, your brother warriors and *me!* You doubted *me!*"

"I will die as an Apache should," Lagarto said steeling himself for the worst. "But first I would ask forgiveness from all of you. I hope you draw strength from my death."

"You owe a debt, there is no doubt," El Mesias said. "However it won't be necessary to pay it with your life."

Lagarto, surprised, looked up with widening eyes. "What do you speak of, El Mesias?"

"You were once an intimate with Tom Fletcher—the White-Eyes our traitors call Cuchillo Largo in the mistaken idea that he has become one of us."

"Yes," Lagarto acknowledged. "I know him well."

"If you went to the Duro Mountains and said you had grown tired of us and no longer believed in us, he would accept your words as truth, no?"

"Yes," Lagarto answered. "But I do not—"

"And you two would become friends again," El Mesias continued. "You would eat together, speak together, even go hunting together."

"Yes," Lagarto said.

"And if he went hunting with you, perhaps you two would go alone with no one else along," El Mesias said.

"We have done that many times," Lagarto said, puzzled.

"Then, if you wish Thunder Eagle's forgiveness, you must perform an important task," El Mesias said.

"I am to return to Tom Fletcher?" Lagarto asked.

"Yes. Win his confidence. Tell him you no longer follow our path. Become his friend again. Go hunting with him alone. And when you are able, take him prisoner and bring him back here for a slow, roasting death."

Lagarto's eyes glistened with grateful tears. "Oh, yes, El Mesias. I will do it. Please, let me have this honor."

El Mesias smiled to himself as others cut the young warrior free from the stakes. Soon Thomas Fletcher would be spread-eagled there, a fire burning brightly on his exposed belly.

* * *

The gaudy sordidness of Nogales contrasted sharply with the usual environment *Capitán* Francisco Moreno endured in his duties with the *Rurales*. The noisy, crowded streets where vendors hawked their wares in a loud sing-song chant seemed stifling to a man used to loads of space. He quickly urged his horse through the throng of the plaza and then turned off to halt in front of the *Comandancia de Rurales*—the Rurale Headquarters.

Another notable difference for Moreno was seeing sharply uniformed *rurales* standing at near ceremonial guard posts around the building. He looked up startled as one quickly presented arms to him in short, snappy movements. Moreno, dust covered and weary, returned the salute with a feeling of self-consciousness as he entered through a large door.

"*Sí, Capitán?*" A neatly uniformed corporal stood up behind a desk and greeted him.

"I am *Capitán* Moreno of *Batallon el Trecero*. I am here to see *Comandante* Platas."

"*Un momentito, mi Capitán,*" the corporal said. The young NCO disappeared through a nearby doorway for several moments. Then he returned and stood at a correct position of attention. "*El Comandante* awaits your presence, *mi Capitán.*"

Moreno nodded curtly thinking how this city boy must spend the evenings spinning wild tales of adventure in the *Rurales* to impress his girl.

Comandante Platas greeted his subordinate with a wide smile. He ignored the salute and stood up offering his hand. "How are you, Moreno? We've had many fine reports of your vigorous enforcement of the Republic's law in the desert."

"*Gracias, mi Comandante,*" Moreno said. "And I am here to discuss such activities out there in the wasteland."

"Of course! But some tequila, eh?" Platas suggested. "A long ride builds a deep thirst, no?"

"Thank you, *Comandante,*" Moreno said.

The older officer tinkled a little bell on his desk and the corporal immediately made an appearance, bearing a tray that held a bottle of the fiery drink along with two glasses, sliced lemon and a small bowl of salt. The two officers went through the ritualistic drinking of tequila by first licking their hands between the thumb and forefinger and depositing a bit of salt there. Then, again licking, they took the salt, a quick shot of the liquor, following this with a suck on the lemon. With this first, most formal, drink out of the way, they settled into small talk for several more relaxing jolts of the Mexican alcohol before Platas thought it proper to get to the business at hand.

"And what brings you to the *Comandancia*, Moreno?"

"I have the sadness to report my garrison has been destroyed by Apaches," Moreno said. "Thankfully the bulk of the men were out on operations with me and only a token force was wiped out. Nonetheless, it appears some were burned alive."

"*¡Bastardos!*" Platas swore.

"Also I must tell you that the bandit chief Chaparro is again on the rampage," Moreno added.

Platas shrugged. "We hear he is fighting these very same Apaches who attacked and destroyed your post."

"He is attacking Apaches, yes," Moreno said, "but only a peaceful band who are in no way connected with the crimes being committed by El Mesias."

"Ah, yes, El Mesias," Platas mused. "We know of him, of course, and we are convinced that is who Chaparro is fighting."

"He will fight him later . . . with United States troops who are even now illegally campaigning in Mexican territory," Moreno said.

"Unsubstantiated," Platas said with a smile.

"I am here to substantiate it, *Comandante*," Moreno said. "I have seen the *gringos* and spoken with them."

"You are mistaken," Platas said calmly.

"No, *Comandante*," Moreno insisted. "I tell you—"

"*You are mistaken!*"

Moreno hesitated, then breathed a despairing sigh. "I understand."

"Good," Platas said. "Now I suggest you return to your garrison and rebuild it as quickly as possible. *Do nothing else!* You are to make no moves against Chaparro or the Apaches, *comprende?*"

Moreno's face twitched in agitation. "*Sí, mi Comandante*," he said. "It would be a shame if my detachment destroyed the Apache marauders and deprived Chaparro of the price of their scalps, no?"

The senior officer ignored the sarcasm. "You are excused, *Capitán*."

Moreno saluted, then left the office with no further ceremony. When he reached his horse, he paused before mounting. It was obvious that chaparro had greased many palms, clear up to and including *Comandante* Platas. And even he, Moreno, had been removed from active operations in the area with the curt order to put the *Fortaleza* back into order.

Now Tanaka Tom Fletcher and the Apaches in the Duro Mountains had lost their one and only ally.

Chapter Fifteen

The two warriors flung Lagarto to the ground. He tried to stand up, but he was once again wrestled to the ground and pinned to the dust.

Tanaka Tom Long Knife, Osote and Guerrero stood over the youth as a stern trio. Their faces were expressionless, but three sets of angry eyes betrayed the disapproval they felt for the warrior.

"What brings you back to us?" Osote asked. "As a Valbajo you have caused me great shame."

Lagarto bowed his head. "It is I who feel shame and remorse, Osote. Toward you and our people—all those who live on the Ancha Mesa—and to my friend and teacher Cuchillo Largo."

Tanaka Tom, ever vigilant, noted the rope marks on Lagarto's wrists and ankles. "Have you been punished by El Mesias?"

"Yes," Lagarto said. "Many times. He is destroying the war party he leads, Cuchillo Largo. He breaks every rule you have taught us about fighting. Too many warriors die for too few gains. When I told him this, he had me staked out to die."

"How did you escape?" Guerrero asked.

"One of the warriors who tied me down is a good friend," Lagarto lied. "He made sure my right hand was loose enough for me to escape. During the night I slipped it free and untied myself. Then I sneaked my pony away from camp, jumped on its back and rode up here."

"And what are we to do with you?" Osote asked sarcastically. "We have too little food now."

"I am a good hunter," Lagarto said. "You remember I was one of the best. Even as a young boy I displayed greater skill than some of the older warriors."

"That is true," Osote said.

"If anybody can find game, I can," Lagarto said eagerly.

"Very well," Osote said. "You go away now. If you come back with meat for us, you can stay. If you have bad luck in your hunting, never come back."

"I will go," Lagarto said, getting to his feet. "But I would ask the honor of having my good friend and teacher Cuchillo Largo go with me. Then I will feel better as our friendship grows again and nurtures itself."

"Would you go with this puppy?" Guerrero asked.

Tanaka Tom nodded his agreement. "Perhaps our camaraderie will prove to be like a broken chain . . . the damaged link reforged through the good hunting that will provide food for the people."

Lagarto yelped his joy. "Let us go now, Cuchillo Largo!"

"I will get my things," Tanaka Tom said. "Wait for me."

As the Six-gun Samurai walked away, Lagarto continued to smile in near boyish delight, but a close examination of his eyes would have revealed them narrowed in murderous anticipation.

Tanaka Tom Long Knife and Lagarto had spent the previous afternoon and early evening wandering fruitlessly in the area of the Duro Mountains in a vain attempt to locate signs of game. Finally with the daylight waning, they settled down in a cold camp to talk, doze, and wait for the coming of a new day.

Now, without eating, they moved off, away from the base of the mountains toward the scrub area that was neither mountain nor desert, a sort of middleground that showed the best—and the worst—of both terrains.

"Cuchillo Largo!" Lagarto's hoarse whisper floated across the distance between himself and the samurai.

Tanaka Tom trotted noiselessly up to the Apache. "What is it?"

"A herd of small deer," Lagarto said, pointing to the ground. He picked up a small ball of feces and smashed it between his fingers, then he sniffed it. "They're very

136

close. It's been less than an hour since they wandered through here."

"If they're grazing then they may be closer than we think."

"If we get enough we can have a regular feast," Lagarto said. "And dancing too. It's been a long time since I have had a chance to flirt with the girls."

Tanaka Tom slipped the Japanese bow off his shoulder. The large, strange instrument with the center of pull a third above the bottom rather than in the center as in western models, was as much a part of the Six-gun Samurai's being as his arms and legs.

It took the pair more than an hour to cover but a short distance. Each step they took had to be a deliberate, careful maneuver as they watched for dry twigs or other vegetation that might crack under their weight and give them away. All this while maintaining a silent vigil on the wind's direction as they circled widely to keep downwind from the deer.

Finally Tom spotted the animals feeding on some thorny plants a hundred yards away. He spent several long moments studying the herd to determine the number and sizes. They were small, but the half dozen little deer would do more than fill the shrunken bellies of the people back in the desolate camp in the mountains. Their morale as well as their health would climb with this nourishment.

Tom moved forward slowly, halting now and then to make sure he wasn't becoming too eager. He edged through the brush, sensing Lagarto close behind, the young Apache seemingly as eager for this kill as he.

At last he reached the right position. Tom paused only for several deep breaths before he reached back and drew the first arrow from the quiver. He set it firmly in place and drew back on the string as he brought the bow up into shooting position. The picture of the deer in front of him suddenly exploded in bright lights at the same instant the numbing pain between his shoulder blades grasped him in an iron grip.

Tanaka Tom staggered to his feet, dazed and confused. He felt consciousness slip away.

137

Lagarto grinned evilly. "That is something you taught me, Cuchillo Largo," he said. "A quick blow to the upper portion of the back in an unexpected manner brings a painful drowsiness. And I also remember what you said about a knuckle driven into the spot just above the belly."

Blackness poured over Tanaka Tom's awareness as Lagarto drove his knuckle deep into the region of his solar plexus.

Tanaka Tom's feet hit the sand as he was pulled from the saddle, and he was able to maintain his balance only for an instant before he sprawled out at the feet of El Mesias.

"Greetings, Thomas Fletcher," the young Apache leader said. "And welcome to the war camp of the Thunder Eagles."

Tom said nothing. Instead he rolled over and started to get at least to his knees. A vicious kick from El Mesias bowled him over to the ground once again.

"You will make no moves without my permission, Thomas Fletcher," El Mesias said. "You are now my prisoner, and as such you are subject to my every whim and command. Do you understand?"

In answer Tom turned face down in the dirt and groaned. Besides the persistent pain in both his chest and back, he had endured a long ride slung over the saddle of his Morgan stallion. Despite his strong constitution and mental control, he had vomited in dry heaves at least a half-dozen times during the bouncy journey.

"Drag him to his feet!" El Mesias' persistent voice cut through Tom's thoughts as two husky warriors grasped him and yanked him to an unsteady standing position. El Mesias looked at his prisoner with contempt. "See him, Thunder Eagles! Observe this interloper who dared pretend he was an Ancha Mesa Apache. Such insolence deserves the longest, slowest death we can devise."

"Hang him head down over a fire!" someone hollered. Yelps of agreement echoed around the camp.

"That is too fast," El Mesias said grinning.

"Cut off his eyelids and bury him up to his neck facing the sun," another suggested.

138

El Mesías cackled his approval. "Now you are showing imagination, Thunder Eagles." He glared his hatred straight into Tanaka Tom's face. "Think of your terrible fate, Thomas Fletcher. They tell me that you believe you have lived many lives before this one. I wonder what heinous misdeed you committed during a previous life on earth to deserve the horrible demise you are about to suffer."

That same thought had already passed through Tanaka Tom's own mind as he observed the naked hatred directed at him from the warriors who had once looked up to him as their leader.

Chapter Sixteen

Cramped muscles and spasms marked the next day's beginning for the Six-gun Samurai. Spread-eagled between stakes, his wrists and ankles were tightly bound by strips of rawhide, and, to add to the discomfort, the Apaches had shoved small stones under his back so that the sharp, persistent pressures kept him awake all through the night.

Tanaka Tom glanced around the camp to get his bearing in the weak dawn light. Most of the warriors still slept, while lookouts huddled in blankets against the predaylight chill, keeping a wary vigil for any possible raiders. The crunch of sand gave away someone approaching him, but the samurai could not twist his head enough to see who it was.

"Who are you?" The voice seemed strangely subdued and peaceful in the armed encampment.

"I am Thomas Fletcher," he replied. "May I inquire as to your identity? I cannot see you."

"Oh! I'm very sorry." The stranger walked around the prostrate prisoner. "I am Solomon Sonador."

Tanaka Tom's remarkable self-control, developed from years of faithfully following *Bushido*, caused him only to open his eyes a bit wider despite the stunning surprise at seeing El Mesias looking down on him. The wild glint of rage that usually danced in the young Indian's dark eyes was gone. Instead his entire countenance seemed placid and unemotional.

"What did you say your name is?" Tom asked again.

"Solomon Sonador," the other replied. "Why are you tied up like that?"

"It is a mistake," Tom answered. "Would you untie me . . . please?"

"Certainly," Sonador replied. He knelt down and worked at the leather binding holding one ankle. "My! These knots certainly are tight."

"Rawhide," Tanaka Tom said in way of explanation. "The night dew causes them to shrink and grow tighter."

"I see," Sonador said as his long, thin fingers pulled at the bonds. Suddenly his efforts slowed—then ceased altogether. His gaze went from his task to Tom's face. The Apache's own expression slowly changed as the eyes narrowed and the mouth drew tight in a scowl. Abruptly he leaped to his feet. "Oh, no! *He* won't free you, Thomas Fletcher. I am stronger than *him!*"

"What?" Tom asked. "I don't understand you."

"That weakling Solomon was about to liberate you, but I, El Mesias, have returned just in time. You won't escape our justice, you impostor!"

Tom sensed the insanity that had returned to El Mesias' being. Clearly two people occupied the Indian's body. He had heard of such a man who roamed the outskirts of Edo. At times this individual was a peaceful Buddhist monk who spent his time praying, meditating or begging for alms at the roadside. But during periods when an alter ego dominated his body, the monk became a despicable *ronin*— a masterless samurai—who committed unspeakable crimes of murder, rape and robbery on unwary travelers. Unfortunately for the personality of the monk, when a special task force of the Shogun's elite bodyguard finally captured and killed the *ronin,* he died too.

El Mesias kicked Tom in the side leaving a painful

140

bruise. "You'll pay for this treachery, Fletcher!" He turned to the guards. "Wake up the camp! We must begin our day now!"

The sentries quickly responded as they went about nudging the other warriors awake. Within five minutes the entire war party was awake and fully armed.

El Mesias pointed to Tom. "This evil White-Eyes attempted to use bad medicine on me. He chanted some sort of magic to push me away and let another rule my body. But Thunder Eagle saw what was happening and came to help me."

The braves, although confused about the exact meaning of their leader's words, cheered this apparent victory nonetheless.

"And while he spoke to me, our great war god said we were to have a double celebration. We are to go on another raiding party and enjoy victory once again as we fight our enemies. When we return we are to send this interloper Fletcher into the world of death!"

The thought of fighting and the possibility of getting women once again excited the Apaches. With arms raised above their heads, they shouted the glory of El Mesias and Thunder Eagle to the heavens above. Then at a signal from Lagarto, they rushed to paint themselves and ready their ponies for the adventure ahead.

El Mesias turned his attention back to Tom. "Enjoy these final moments, Thomas Fletcher. Before this day is out, those distant hills will play the echoes of your screams!" He delivered another vicious kick before turning away to his own preparations for the warpath.

Within an hour the camp had emptied of all except the prisoner and the two warriors detailed to guard him. Tanaka Tom endured both verbal and physical abuse from the two who were disgruntled about being left behind. Finally they grew bored and drew off to one side to await the return of their more fortunate comrades.

The samurai took advantage of this solitude to withdraw deep into himself and concentrate his entire energy and life flow to his *hara*—that point in the abdomen where a man's veritable center of life and strength is located. Tanaka Tom breathed deeply, eyes tightly closed, letting his *ki*—the life's vibrations—build up in the sacred place. Each breath grew considerably longer and deeper until his spirit and all effort was finely tuned, ready to be put to the use he had for it.

Strength flowed up through his chest and shoulders, then eased to his wrists and hands as a slow but strong current of water might follow a natural channel in the earth. Alertness and a sense of growing strength blossomed until he felt invincible. One more deep breath and an explosion of energy hit his hands like a bolt of lightning.

The stakes flew upward from the dirt as Tanaka Tom sat up. Two quick pulls and the rawhide holding his feet parted as if made of tissue paper. In another single, smooth movement he was on his feet, moving toward his horse where his saddle and other belongings were stacked.

The two guards, astounded at the amazing sight their eyes refused to believe, hesitated in their surprise and were not able to move until the samurai had reached his gear. The *katana's* blade flashed in the morning sun as it seemed to leap from its scabbard into Tanaka Tom's hands.

The first Apache who reached the samurai, attacked holding his tomahawk high for a quick slash to the head. Tanaka Tom brought his sword up in a graceful arc cutting off the hand holding the weapon. Then, spinning completely around on his heel, he sent the blade slicing through the assailant's abdomen spilling intestines to the sand.

All this before the Indian had time to utter even an astonished scream.

By this time the second attacker had arrived with his lance. Tanaka Tom feigned an attack, then took one hand from the sword handle and grasped the spearlike weapon and pulled it along with the momentum of the attack. He suddenly reversed his movement, raising the lance up and back. The Apache's legs kept running as he tipped backward until he twisted in a desperate attempt to retain his balance.

The *katana* blade whistled through the air once again,

142

this time dumping a head onto the desert terrain. The decapitated body writhed and kicked for several minutes until, like the other, it lay still and dead.

Tom quickly saddled the Morgan, arranged his gear, and galloped from the camp back toward the Duro Mountains.

* * *

Roberto Orlando wiped at the sweat that trickled from his *sombrero*. He had once been Chaparro's number one bodyguard, but since the escape of that *bastardo* Fletcher, he had been demoted. Finally Chaparro had given him another chance to prove himself and get back into his good graces. All Orlando had to do was take a half-dozen *bandidos* out, then locate and capture Thomas Fletcher alive. Although he knew the chances of success were nil, Orlando wanted so much to get back into his chief's good graces that he would have tried to find hell and capture the devil himself if he had been ordered to.

The bandit had spent almost two weeks scouting around the Duro Mountains for signs of the elusive *gringo*. He had found out his quarry had gone off hunting with one of the Apaches, but by the time the Mexicans had cut the trail, it was too cold to do them any good.

But now just hours previously, he had received a report that Fletcher was out on the desert and heading back toward the Duros. There was only one reasonable trail up to the Apache camp, so Orlando had laid out a hasty ambush and emphasized to his men that he wanted the *Americano* alive. Any *hijo de la chingada* who shot or knifed the swordsman would pay dearly for disobeying orders.

Now, from his vantage point atop a boulder overlooking the trail, Orlando could barely make out the lone rider approaching them.

A half-hour later, there was no doubt it was Thomas Fletcher.

Orlando motioned to his men to keep down as he crept out farther on his boulder. He waited patiently for Tanaka Tom to ride closer . . . closer . . . closer.

143

When he judged the time was right, he leaped.

His calculations were off but a half-second, and instead of striking Fletcher directly the Mexican hit the Morgan's rump. He had enough presence of mind to reach out and drag the American down with him as he bounced off the horse.

Tanaka Tom could see his mount gallop away as he fell with Orlando's arm tightly around his neck. He had but an instant to regret that his *katana* and other weapons had been hastily attached to the saddle before he collided with the ground.

Weaponless, but ready, the samurai rolled to his feet and stood facing the dazed Orlando. The sounds around him caused Tom to glance up and note the six other *bandidos* who now warily approached him.

Orlando slowly stood up with a glazed expression. Finally he recovered enough to speak. "Put up your hands, *gringo,* we're taking you back to Chaparro."

Tanaka Tom shook his head. "Not on your life. Chaparro will have me shot anyhow. I would prefer to die here fighting than be tied to a stake for your leader's amusement."

"*¡Vámanos, muchachos!*" Orlando shouted. He rushed the samurai who caught his wrist in both hands. Then, after pivoting on his heel, Tanaka Tom brought the Mexican over his shoulder and threw him hard to the ground. A quick *ka-soku-tei* heel stamp to the head and Orlando's tortilla chomping days ended for good.

A second *bandido* leaped onto Tom's back exactly at the same time another hit him from the front in a spontaneous but uncoordinated attack. Tom staggered under the double weight as the other four moved in with punches and kicks. Many of these blows rained on their two *camaradas* who hung onto the gyrating, whirling samurai for dear life, but Tom was catching enough to hurt him as the six assailants kept up the persistent attack.

Finally, Tanaka Tom Long Knife, bruised and dazed, collapsed under the frenzied assault.

He tried to recover but a fist slammed into his left

temple so hard his vision blurred. Once again Tanaka Tom made an effort to keep up the fight, but several more head blows made what little consciousness he had left reel and slip away. He did manage to regain his feet once, but his legs turned to jelly and he fell back as the bandits, laughing and jeering, gathered around to tie him up and take him back to Chaparro.

The first shot slammed into one *bandido's* back, while the second smashed the face of another.

The other four looked around long enough for two more of their number to buckle under the carbine slugs. The survivors turned to run, but one leaped up from the impact of a back shot as the other scampered to safety in the boulders.

Paloma, the Spencer's bore smoking, stepped out from the cover of the upper trail. She had spent the previous two days there waiting for her man to return. She had little trust for Lagarto and had sensed treachery on his part. If not allowed to accompany a hunting party because she was a mere woman, she could at least get far enough away from camp to meet her man on his way back. She had observed the attack on Tanaka Tom Long Knife from above and had descended to a closer range to rescue him.

The Apache woman rushed out to where Tom now sat up in his efforts to recover from the savagery he had endured from the *bandidos*. He had barely sensed the shots that had rescued him, but even his befuddled mind could comprehend what had happened when he saw Paloma walking up with the weapon in her hand. He had only time to speak once before he passed out.

"Gracias, mujer mía."

* * *

Captain Terrance MacNally sat on the crude campstool and took angry sips of coffee from the clay mug provided by his host. "I'm certain we can work out our difficulties," he said after finishing off the hot drink. "It's to both our advantages even if we approach the problem from different angles."

145

"Certainly," Chaparro agreed. He glanced out to where MacNally's troopers were bivouacked. More than two dozen *bandidos* had been stationed in inconspicuous lookout areas in case the *gringo* captain attempted any treachery. "But I want to make sure I can get enough scalps for my efforts in this endeavor to be profitable."

"I am willing to let you have every Indian cadaver whether killed by your men or mine," MacNally assured him. "You can mutilate them to your heart's desire . . . I don't give a damn. And I'm not concerned whether it is you or I who executes that bastard Fletcher. I only want to see the job done—and properly!"

"Then I will perform those honors," Chaparro said. "You are, of course, invited to the ceremony."

"Then we should be in complete agreement," MacNally said.

"We are," Chaparro remarked. "Except for the methods we wish to employ. You are too anxious to wipe out the *indios* in the Duro Mountains, *Capitán*."

"I said you can have their goddamned scalps!" MacNally hissed.

"And I appreciate that," Chaparro said. "But if you destroy that group, then the warparty will be alerted. Then they will either go back up north where I can't get to them, or their leader will become more wily and difficult to corner."

"I can assure you they will not go back to the United States," MacNally said. "Their only sanctuary is the Ancha Mesa and there are many troops around there now. They could never reach safety there."

"Even if they stayed in Mexico, they will be harder to catch if they know there are many of us after them," Chaparro insisted. "It will cost me a lot of men."

"Casualties are to be expected in an undertaking of this sort," MacNally replied with cold-blooded logic.

"Unfortunately for me I do not have recruiting stations to supply me with replacements like you do," Chaparro argued. "My men are from families that have been with this bandit group for generations. Each loss we suffer cannot be replaced until a boy grows into a man."

"Surely there's enough cutthroats in this part of the country to provide you with the number of fighters you need," MacNally said.

"But the quality of such riffraff does not match that of our own people, born and raised in our traditions," Chaparro said. "As a soldier I'm sure you can appreciate that."

MacNally had to admit his agreement to himself. Family and fraternal ties were invaluable in a fighting organization. Despite their simplicity and crudity, Chaparro's men had rough traditions that ran as deeply as those of any spit-and-polish army regiment.

"But if—" MacNally said as he was interrupted.

"¡Jefe! ¡Jefe!" a bandit shouted, running up to where the two were talking. "One of the men who went with Orlando to the Duros is returning. He just rode into camp."

"Fetch him to me immediately," Chaparro ordered.

MacNally, who had not been able to follow the rapid exchange of Spanish looked puzzled. "What's going on?"

"One of the men from the scouting party is back," Chaparro said. "Orlando may have sent him with news."

"Well, I hope it's good," MacNally fumed.

"We shall see," Chaparro said.

Moments later a disheveled *bandido* brought his lathered horse to a stop in front of his chief. He dismounted and held onto the reins. "Everyone is dead but me, *mi jefe*."

"What happened?" Chaparro asked.

"The swordsman was spotted and Orlando had us set up an ambush," the man explained. "We were successful and had him in our grasp, but—"

"¡Chingado!" Chaparro swore. "But what?"

"We were attacked by an overwhelming group of Apaches, *jefe mío*," the bandit exaggerated. "The other *muchachos* fell like flies within an instant. Only through the blessings of the *Virgin de Guadalupe* did I manage to escape."

"Save your miserable blaspheming of Mexico's sainted lady," Chaparro said irritated. "What became of Fletcher?"

"He was taken back up into the Duro Mountains," the man said.

MacNally leaped to his feet. "Then that's where that bastard is right now! Those goddamned Apaches have been up in that godforsaken place long enough to be half-starved by now. I'm going up there and smash 'em once and for all."

Before Chaparro could react, the American officer was gone and within minutes bugle calls had set the cavalry troopers stirring to action.

One of the Mexican guards looked over at his chief. "Are we going to stop them?"

Chaparro shrugged. "What for? It will cost too much time and men. Besides, when he gets his hands on Fletcher, I'm going to take that *bastardo* away from him and string both those *gringos* up by their *huevos!*"

The guard laughed his agreement and encouragement. "*Asi es mi jefe!*"

Chapter Seventeen

"Come on you slugs! Keep moving!" Sergeant Stensland urged the men. The small team of troopers did their best to hurry the pace as they edged up higher into the rocky hill that held the Apache camp on its summit.

Below Captain MacNally and Lieutenant Richard Martin watched through binoculars the progress of two dozen similar groups slowly working their way through the rocks as they ascended the barren mountain. "That's the only way to assault such a natural fortress," MacNally said. "A strong frontal attack would only result in heavy losses. But the use of small independent teams sneaking through the defenses will have us cracking this tough nut from several different angles."

"A good lesson in tactics, Sir," Martin said enthusiastically.

"Correct," MacNally said immodestly. "This sort of

campaign should prove invaluable to a young officer like yourself, Mister Martin. In fact, I have no objections if you keep notes.''

"Oh, yes, Sir!" Martin said as he took the hint. He fished a small notebook out of a tunic pocket and immediately began writing in it. "I'm sure I shall refer to this small journal many times during my career, Sir."

"I'm certain that you will," MacNally said. Then he added magnanimously, "If you have any questions, don't hesitate to bring them up to me, Mister Martin."

"Oh, thank you, Sir," Martin said. "I'm sure that I shall."

The duty bugler scampered up to the two officers and saluted. "Special detail comin' in, Sor," the young Irishman said. "And it looks loike they managed to git ahold o' one o' them heathens, Sor."

"Very well, Murphy," MacNally said. He hated the man's brogue. It reminded himself too much of his own poverty-stricken background in a rundown New York Irish neighborhood. The captain had spent years perfecting his accent by the simple dint of raw imitation of his better educated peers.

A corporal, leading four troopers carrying a burden in a blue army blanket, reported in with a flourishing salute. "Sir, Corp'ral Darwin reports to the commandin' officer with a dead Apache."

"Let's have a look at him," MacNally said.

At a nod from the NCO, the soldiers laid the blanket on the ground and folded it back to reveal the body of a young Apache warrior appearing to be in his midteens.

MacNally studied the corpse carefully for several moments. "What do you make of this, Mister Martin?"

"Martin, still not used to viewing the dead, grimaced involuntarily as he looked at the Indian. "He appears rather skinny, Sir, and . . . well, quite dirty and unkempt."

"Of course. What does that indicate?" MacNally asked.

"Ah . . . Sir, I would say he hasn't been eating well lately," Martin said.

149

"Correct, Mister Martin. Those bastards are literally starving up in these mountains. That means they're weak and unsteady. A condition which will affect their mental and fighting capacities as well," MacNally said. "Now what about his unkempt condition?"

"Well, Sir, I'd say this Indian did not bathe at regular intervals," Martin said.

"I doubt if this Indian ever did bathe," MacNally said. "Water is something Apaches don't have much of . . . though up in the Ancha Mesa they may have done some swimming, but I doubt it. Apaches and water sports don't seem to mix well. No, Mister Martin, it's not the dirtiness of his *body* that intrigues me, it's his *hair*. He hasn't cared for it properly. Another sign of dejection and low morale. Something else to our favor, eh?"

"Undoubtedly, Sir!"

"You may enter that in your notebook too, Mister Martin," MacNally said.

"Oh, thank you, Sir!"

As the two officers talked, up above Tanaka Tom worked at organizing a defense against an attack he hadn't expected. Osote, his usual enthusiasm undampened despite the threat, grinned at his friend. "How many horse soldiers will we kill today, Cuchillo Largo?"

"As many as *karma* dictates, old friend," Tom answered. "But first we must learn from where the attack is coming."

"From all over," Guerrero answered trotting up to his friends at that exact moment. "I have been around the edge of the camp, and there is shooting everywhere."

Osote snorted his disgust. "I didn't think there were enough pony soldiers to try to overwhelm us in that fashion. They have gone crazy from the hot sun."

"Perhaps not," Tanaka Tom Long Knife said. "I think I shall have to make a quick survey of this battle before I make any decisions."

A sudden explosion of gunshots at the south side of the camp quickly drew the three stalwarts' attention. They rushed to the area to add their own bullets to those of the warriors stationed there. The soldiers' attack melted away as quickly as it had begun.

"Perhaps it will be an easy battle, Cuchillo Largo," Guerrero said, grinning.

Before the Six-gun Samurai could answer there were more shots sounding to the west. Once again the attack dissolved but another one popped up at another part of the camp's perimeter.

"What's going on?" Osote asked in anger and fear.

"Our soldier friends have grown smart," Tanaka Tom said, as he realized what was going on. "They know a full frontal attack would fail. So they are utilizing patience by wearing us down a little at a time. We lose a warrior here and there, while they lose soldiers in the same way. The only trouble is that there are many, many more soldiers than warriors. In two, maybe three days we will not be much of a fighting force."

"Surely we can beat them at this game," Osote said.

Tanaka Tom shook his head. "We don't stand a chance." Another gunfight popped up, then died away leaving two more warriors lying still in the mountain dirt.

"You don't mean that, Cuchillo Largo," Guerrero said, scoffing. "What a joke you make! You are never discouraged."

Tanaka Tom's solemn expression gave silent testimony to the sincerity of his pessimism. "I have my own way of preparing for death. I suggest you turn to your death songs . . . unless you desire to surrender. My customs, which I call *Bushido*, will not permit me to knowingly or purposefully become a prisoner. I must die."

"You are not going to die," Osote said calmly. "And neither am I. At least not here or now . . . unless a chance bullet catches us."

"Of course not," Guerrero said. "We still have *el alud*."

"*El alud?*" the samurai asked. "What is that?"

Osote pointed up to a ridge just above the camp. "See there? If you look carefully you may note rope and basket netting covering the dirt in front of that pile of boulders."

151

Tanaka Tom's keen eyes had seen the items before. "So? What are they for?" he asked

"There are three places to cut heavy ropes there," Osote explained. "When that is done, most of that ridge will tumble down here on this camp. Anything or anyone beneath it will be crushed by much earth."

"Many years ago our people fixed this as a last defense," Guerrero said. "Even lately we have inspected it and kept it in good shape."

"I saw men working up there before," Tom said. "But I thought they were perhaps looking for places that might make good water holes."

"If we can lure the soldiers up on this mountain and into this spot," Osote said, "we can smash them flat."

"That will be easy if we get everybody up on that ridge," Tom said. "Is there room?"

"It will be crowded," Osote answered. "But everyone will fit."

Guerrero laughed. "Especially as skinny as we are now, eh?"

"Let's get the people moving then," Tanaka Tom suggested. "And make it appear as if they are frightened. That will fool the soldiers into thinking we have panicked and headed for higher ground out of sheer fright."

"*¡Vámonos!*" Guerrero said.

He and Osote began shouting orders that sent the women and children scampering toward the ridge. They carried whatever belongings they could hastily gather up and led the family ponies scrambling up the dry dirt to the top of the ridge.

Tanaka Tom met Paloma, with their child Pumito on her back, as she led the Morgan stallion and mule. The Apache woman grinned at her man in fierce happiness. "Do not worry, *hombre mío*, all your precious belongings are packed on the mule. You will lose nothing."

Tanaka Tom, knowing that his Japanese items were irreplaceable, appreciated her thoughtfulness and efficiency. Although there were wails of grief at losing some valued item, the women and children were soon atop the ridge, waiting for the warriors to join them.

"Listen now!" Tanaka Tom shouted. "Fall back slowly and keep firing at any soldiers you see. But try to get up on the top as quickly as possible."

"Remember *el alud* has been waiting for years to serve our people," Osote reminded them. "We must be careful in drawing the soldiers beneath its awesome weight."

Down below the camp Sergeant Stensland had just decided to lead his men forward again. After scampering through the boulders they found the Indian positions deserted. A quick scout revealed the last of the warriors clawing up the ridge in what seemed a frightened hurry. The sergeant rubbed his grizzled chin. "You slugs stand fast here," he said. "I'm reporting this to Captain MacNally."

The NCO nimbly descended the boulder strewn hill and rushed to his commander. "Sir, them Apaches have holed up on that small ridge above their camp area."

MacNally grinned widely. "Have they deserted their hovels, then?"

"Yes, Sir. We can move through there pretty easy. They didn't give us much of a fight at all," Stensland said. "We mighta been able to git 'em in one rush after all."

"No, Sergeant," MacNally said with a superior grin. "Even in their weakened condition they would have inflicted far more casualties on us than we could have endured. This action is going exactly as I planned it."

"Thank God for that, Sir," Stensland said. "Orders, Sir?"

"Assemble the men just below the village," MacNally said. "We have reached the point where our big attack is now called for."

While the soldiers reassembled for what they planned to be the final rush, Tanaka Tom hastily organized the defense of the ridge.

Osote laughed aloud at his efforts. "Do not worry, Cuchillo Largo, the pony soldiers will not get up to this ridge. It will go to them!"

Tanaka Tom, who knew there was no proper word for

153

"contingency" in the Apache language, only shrugged. "I always prefer to expect the worst."

Guerrero joined in the conversation with a lazy grin. "If you don't move back from the edge of the ridge, the worst will surely happen, Cuchillo Largo. You will tumble down on top of the soldiers."

Tom nodded his understanding, then turned to move back some of the warriors he had posted too far forward. He had little confidence in this last ditch effort of the Apaches and was fully committed to dying among the rocks.

Within a half-hour bugles blared and several skirmish lines of soldiers moved up onto the plateau that held the wickiups. As they passed through the crude dwellings, the troops fired into them or knocked them over. A weak volley from Tanaka Tom and his cohorts only served to speed them up.

"Let them move forward farther," Osote said. "But have the warriors start hacking at the ropes and nets until they are cut halfway through."

The samurai sighed loudly. "These rocks and dirt have been packed in here for years," he said to Osote. "I'm afraid they may have become a solid part of the mountain."

Osote shook his head. "No, Tanaka Tom. We are sitting on a big boulder here. Nothing that rests on it is solid . . . as you will soon see."

Moments later the first line of troops had reached the base of the ridge. Osote raised his arm and lowered it rapidly to signal the cutters to completely sever the rope and netting.

The second line of troops by then were stumbling up the slope as the erratic firing of the defenders did little to stop them. Occasionally a blue-clad figure would lurch and drop to the ground, but the attack still pressed on relentlessly. Then the third and final rank of skirmishers began the climb and an overwhelming number of soldiers now edged up toward the samurai and his friends.

Then the side of the hill lurched and rumbled.

The troops, with the earth shifting around their feet,

154

hesitated and looked to MacNally for some sort of sign. The captain immediately sensed his whole attack was about to be carried away and he turned to the bugler. "Sound *Retreat*, goddammit!" He waved his saber at his men. "Get the hell down from there, quickly! Run like the devil himself was after yez." His Irish brogue jumped back into his voice in the excitement. "Saints preserve us! Them heathen bastards have got this bloody mountain rigged to come down on our heads. Run, lads! Run fer the valley and don't quit 'til yez git there!"

Suddenly the mountain began slipping and this added to the panic. The soldiers threw down rifles, haversacks and anything else that might hinder their flight.

MacNally, his rage overcoming his fear for an instant, stopped and looked up at the ridge. He could see the Six-gun Samurai standing there watching the man-made avalanche roll after the troops. He shook his fist and screamed, "This is the second time ye've done this to me, ye Jappo bastard, but it'll be the last. That I swear to ye!"

The thundering roar increased as the rolling earth gained momentum and buried unlucky soldiers who had been too slow to flee. Within moments the area was totally quiet, the former Apache camp now flattened and empty except for an occasional arm or leg showing where a crushed corpse lay.

"I meant to ask you something," Tanaka Tom said to Osote. "I was unfamiliar with the Spanish word *alud*. But I think I figured it out. It means avalanche, no?"

"It mean avalanche, yes!" Osote said laughing.

Guerrero shouted his triumph so loudly it echoed off the distant hills. "Again we have experienced victory with our friend Cuchillo Largo! Surely Thunder Eagle watches over us."

But Tom's elation was short lived. "Don't forget the other result of using *el alud*," he said to his friends. "It means we are now defenseless."

"Let us hope the pony soldier chief doesn't figure that out," Osote said.

*   *   *

By late evening it was evident that MacNally had indeed withdrawn fully from the area. His demoralized and frightened troops rode out in a weary, dusty column following their commander back to Chaparro's camp where he would try to figure another way to get the elusive Thomas Fletcher.

The object of the captain's rage now rested at his fire in front of a blanket lean-to that Paloma had set up. Osote and Guerrero sat in the dirt across from him, their faces serious as they listened to their friend's counsel.

"We are defeated here," Tanaka Tom said. "We have no help from Moreno or his *Rurales*, there will be no supplies coming our way, ammunition is low, and the people are now starving."

"I know you cannot surrender, Cuchillo Largo, so we will let the people go, then you, Guerrero and I will stay here and fight to the end," Osote said.

"Aaiiyeee!" Guerrero exclaimed. "It will be a glorious death. The Ancha Mesa Apaches will sing of our brave deed forever."

"It will accomplish nothing to do even that glorious a thing," Tanaka Tom said. "I must think of the people anyway. If the *bandidos* get them, they will be butchered for scalps. If they manage to get back to America, they will never see their precious Ancha Mesa again. The U.S. government will send them far away to some awful reservation to starve."

"Then all will die," Osote said.

"I had one idea," Tanaka Tom said. "The three of us are well known because of the trial during the last trouble on the Ancha Mesa.* It would be impressive if we approached the army commander at Fort Bozie and told him the truth of the situation here. Perhaps if he were convinced that El Mesias is the real culprit, the people here would be allowed to return to their traditional homeland to live in peace."

"Why didn't we do that in the first place?" Osote asked with unabashed curiosity.

* See Sixgun Samurai #2: *Bushido Vengeance*, pages 150-162.

"Because there was no pressure we could put on the army," Tom said.

"What pressure do we have now that we didn't before?" Guerrero asked.

"Captain MacNally is here in Mexico illegally. Any hearings or trials that might result from capturing us or any of the Ancha Mesa people might prove embarrassing not only to the army but the United States government."

"Is that important?" Osote asked. The ways of white men never failed to cause him wonder and concern. They would cheerfully cheat and mistreat Indians, in some instances, but when it came to being open and honest about it, they would hem and haw and generally quietly withdraw from the scene like a pack of coyotes from a poisoned waterhole.

Tanaka Tom smiled. "It is most important."

"Then let us go at first light, Cuchillo Largo," Guerrero said.

"Yes," the samurai agreed. "Perhaps only three of us will not attract any attention from soldiers or *bandidos*."

Osote stood up. "I will sing to Spirit Woman for her protection. Pass a peaceful night, friends."

Guerrero left too, then Paloma sat down beside Tanaka Tom. "Do you have great faith in your plan, *hombre mío?*"

"Not much," Tanaka Tom admitted. "But at least it's a chance that cuts down the possibility of total disaster."

"I might not see you for many weeks," Paloma said. She pulled a blanket over the two of them until they were completely covered. "Come into me, Tanaka Tom, and let your seed warm my belly during the cold nights you will be away."

* * *

For most of the day the journey had been uneventful. Tanaka Tom, Osote and Guerrero rode as a loose, spread out group, each keeping a wary eye on the horizon for any possible danger.

The *bandidos* came at sunset.

The Mexicans had been following the three for several hours. They were curious why the trio would be moving north on their own toward the land of the *gringos*. Familiar with *Señor* Fletcher's reputation as a fighter and strategist, they suspected a trap. By the end of the day, they were more afraid the samurai would escape them than they were of any sly tricks, and they launched a wildly yelling, shooting attack that quickly broke down into a chase.

Tanaka Tom and his friends took one quick look before breaking into a wild gallop in the original direction of their journey. Their horses caught the seriousness of the moment and did their best to respond to the urgency of their owners' voices and kicks in the flanks, but the animals, like the men, had been too long underfed to keep up any great physical exertion for very long. They tired quickly and the gap between the *bandido* pursuers and their prey narrowed appreciably and rapidly.

Finally Osote's pony snorted loud and long in protest and simply slowed down on his own. Tom wheeled the Morgan to see what he could do to help, but Osote shook his head.

"This pony will not run," Osote said in anger.

Guerrero edged up to his friend's mount. "A good lash on the rump will make that *perizoso* move, but not long enough."

"You two go on," Osote said. "There is nothing more to be done."

"No!" Guerrero shouted. "The two of *you* ride on. I will stay and fight the *mexicanos* alone."

"You cannot live through such a fight," Tanaka Tom said.

"Then it is a good day to die," Guerrero said. "And what is that word you use all the time to describe men's fates?"

"*Karma*," Tom replied.

"Then whatever happens to me here today is my *karma*," Guerrero said calmly. He suddenly slapped his pony lash down hard on Osote's horse. The animal whinnied in pain and anger, but bolted away into a gallop toward the north.

Guerrero nodded to the samurai. "Follow him, friend. If this *karma* you mention is kind to me we shall meet again in this world. If not I shall be with Spirit Woman tonight. *Adiós!*"

. Tom, realizing the urgency of the situation, pulled on the reins of his stallion. *"Adiós!"* As he pounded toward Osote's disappearing figure, he turned back for a last glance at Guerrero who was settling in to face the *bandidos.* Tanaka Tom took time to wave a final farewell. *"Adiós, Apache samurai!"*

Chapter Eighteen

The first thing the sentry did when Tanaka Tom and Osote rode up to the gate of Fort Bozie, Arizona Territory, was to call the Corporal of the Guard.

That NCO surveyed the pair nervously and summoned the august presence of the Sergeant of the Guard.

The sergeant was just as perplexed and sent a nearby soldier scrambling for the Officer of the Day.

The Officer of the Day, a nervous young second lieutenant, went them a step better and called out the entire guard to escort the visitors to post headquarters.

After running the gamut through the sergeant major and the adjutant, Tanaka Tom Fletcher and Osote finally stood before the desk of the commanding officer, Colonel Orville Breckenridge.

The old colonel was confused.

"By God . . . er, that is to say, you're Thomas Fletcher, aren't you?" the colonel asked.

"Yes," Tanaka Tom answered. "And I'm sure you remember my friend Osote of the Ancha Mesa Apaches."

"Yes, by God! He was one of the Indians on trial with you in Lone Gap!"

"Correct, Sir."

Breckenridge began to gain some control and his blustering eased as he leaned back in his chair. "Well, now, why have you come calling on me, Mister Fletcher? Although you're not officially wanted, I believe I have grounds to hold you on federal charges involving the campaign against the Ancha Mesa Apaches."

"Perhaps, Sir," Tom admitted. "But the charges would be unfounded. My reason for being here is to explain the real situation and inform you about the true culprits in the crimes being blamed on my friends."

"I'm going to consider this an inquiry of sorts," Breckenridge interrupted. He called out for his adjutant who rushed in immediately. The colonel snorted his approval at the haste shown in his behalf. "Get Private Young and have him report here immediately."

"Yes, Sir!" The officer spun on his heel and rushed out shouting. "Sergeant Major! Get Private Young to report to the colonel immediately!"

"Yes, Sir!" a more distant voice echoed. "Corporal Tomkins, get Young to report to commandin' officer *now!* NOW!"

A voice even farther away could be heard yelling around the garrison yard. "Young! Young! Get yore ass into the old man's office *pronto,* godammit, or I'll slam it up between yore ears!"

Within ten minutes a slim, almost effeminate young man wearing spectacles appeared timidly at the door of the colonel's office. He knocked lightly.

"Come in, Young," Breckenridge said.

"Sir, Private Young reporting as ordered," he said, saluting.

"Make yourself comfortable," the colonel said. "I have work for you." The officer turned to Tom Fletcher. "This young man is rather talented at shorthand, Mister Fletcher. He'll record our conversation here."

"Excellent," Tom said, voicing his approval. The more witnesses and paperwork on what he had to say, the better, as far as the samurai was concerned.

"Very well," Breckenridge said, after Young had settled down with pad and pencils. "I believe you, Mister Thomas Fletcher, wish to make a statement regarding the crimes being committed by the Ancha Mesa Apaches."

"Certain elements of those clans, Colonel," Tom said correcting him. "A young Indian leader El Mesias has organized a warrior society of Ancha Mesa braves and is currently raiding and making war in Mexico. . . ." Tom continued his narrative bringing in El Mesias' true name of Solomon Sonador. He told of several outrages he knew were committed in Arizona Territory, and he cited the fact that the great majority of the Apaches were not involved in these activities but were chased relentlessly and unlawfully from their legal homelands through the efforts of a certain Captain Terrance James MacNally.

Breckenridge interrupted with a loud cough. "Now see here, Fletcher! MacNally is acting under my direct orders."

"Are you having the statement put in the records, Colonel?" Tanaka Tom asked.

"Of course! Read it back to us, Young," the colonel ordered.

"Yes, Sir . . . 'Now see here, Fletcher. MacNally is acting under my direct orders.' "

"Does that include operating across the border in the Mexican Republic, Colonel?" Tom asked.

"Of course not!"

"Well, Sir, that's exactly where he is."

"I . . . he couldn't . . . that's in violation . . . goddammit! Young, stop taking notes!" Breckenridge said. Then he recovered momentarily. "You have no evidence of such a flagrant disregard for international law, Fletcher."

"Indeed I do, Colonel," Tanaka Tom said. "Captain Francisco Moreno, an officer of the Mexican *Rurale* force, has met face-to-face with Captain MacNally across the border. Not only did your officer refuse to leave Mexico, he threatened this Mexican official if he dared interfere with his plans or activities."

Breckenridge sputtered, then broke into a coughing fit, his face turning purple as he hacked helplessly. Finally the adjutant appeared with a glass of water.

161

"It's a serious situation," Tanaka Tom said after the colonel recovered somewhat. "But I think it can be ironed out to everyone's satisfaction without any official notice being taken. That's a polite way of saying no one will get into trouble."

"I know what you mean!" Breckenridge snapped. He darted an angry glance at Young. "Are you taking notes?"

"No, sir," the young man answered in a quaking voice. "You told me—"

"Get the hell out of here, you wimpy little bastard!" Breckenridge shrieked. "And take your goddamned pad and pencils with you!"

The young soldier fled from the office.

"I'm open for any suggestions from you," Tanaka Tom said calmly. "This thing is already too deep to ignore. Not only is that young man aware of the violation perpetrated by Captain MacNally, but I'm sure others in the outer office heard me too."

"It cannot be hidden, I'll admit," Breckenridge said sullenly. He could see thirty-five years of hard soldiering ending with a stretch in a federal prison . . . or being stripped of his commission . . . or the loss of his pension. "I'll tell you what, Fletcher. I'll write orders—witnessed by my adjutant and two other officers—directing Captain MacNally to proceed back to this side of the border. I will tell him to terminate any active campaigning and report to me immediately."

"I'm not concerned about MacNally's location," Tanaka Tom said coldly.

"I'm not finished, Fletcher. I'll also call off any more activities directed against the Ancha Mesa people. They may return unmolested to their homes here in Arizona. And I'll consult you regarding any action directed against this warrior society you told me about."

Tanaka Tom looked at Osote and smiled widely. The Indian sensed the victory and nodded his approval. The samurai turned back to the colonel. "How soon may I have that order, Colonel?"

"Right now," the colonel said. He looked around. "Now

where in hell did Young get off to." He hollered out to the outer office. "Adjutant, fetch Private Young immediately!"

Tanaka Tom grinned to himself as the relay of yelling began again.

Within an hour the samurai and Apache warrior rode out of Fort Bozie and turned south for Mexico. Osote was happy beyond words. "Do we go to the Duros for our people now, Cuchillo Largo?"

"No," Tanaka Tom said. "I don't trust MacNally to follow these orders. We'll look up our friend Francisco Moreno in Nogales. Perhaps he can supply us with a few *Rurales* to guarantee protection against bandits *and* Captain Terrance MacNally."

Francisco Moreno's joy at seeing his friend Thomas Fletcher was so great it cleared the tequila fumes from his brain in a few moments. The *Rurale* officer sat up on his bunk and let the dizziness evaporate before he lurched to his feet and grasped Tom in a Latin embrace. "How are you, *compañero?* It is good to see a man of action again after sitting around here in this town of soft asses."

"If you're bored I have a suggestion to remedy that," Tom said, getting to the point. He showed Moreno the orders from Breckenridge to be delivered to MacNally.

"That will get that *gringo* bastard out of my hair," Moreno said happily. "But I still must deal with Chaparro in some way."

"If you can get enough men to help me escort the Ancha Mesa people safely through Sonora and to the border, I will give you my personal help in dealing with the bandit chief."

Moreno laughed. "With you it will be like a hundred men, *amigo.*" He thought deeply for several moments. "I can make my superiors—and my men too—think that I am taking my detachment out for some field exercises to toughen them up. Once they are away from Nogales I will be back in control again."

"Then we can wrap this situation up pretty and proper," Tanaka Tom said.

163

"¡Seguro! And when I kill that *bastardo* Chaparro, my *comandante* will not dare chastise me. To do so would be to admit he's been taking bribes from that stinking *bandido*." Moreno laughed aloud. "He will have to give me a medal and sing my praises to the sky—all this through teeth clenched in anger. ¡*Chihuahua*! What a beautiful picture to imagine!"

As Tanaka Tom and Moreno made their plans, Corporal Oscar Gomez, the *Rurale* who had carried the information of Tom's release to Chaparro, seemingly dozed, as he did every day, near his commander's window. The corporal now received pay from two sources: one, the Mexican government for his services as a rural policeman; and two, from Chaparro the bandit chief as an informer. The enterprising young man had made it a point to always be near during any official hubbub in the garrison. He knew this new information about Moreno and Fletcher getting the Apaches out of the Duro Mountains would be well received by the *bandidos*.

Gomez, seemingly calm but with a stomach full of butterflies, ambled across the stable yard and saddled his horse without attracting too much attention from the other *rurales* nearby.

He mounted tha animal and let it slowly walk out through the barracks gate before he turned toward the outskirts of town.

Once clear of Nogales, he dug the cruel Mexican spurs into the horse's flank and rode hell-for-leather toward Chaparro's camp.

* * *

Four hours of hard riding found *Cabo* Oscar Gomez standing near exhaustion in front of Chaparro. He told the bandit chief of Tanaka Tom's and Moreno's plan for dealing with the *bandidos* and the Apaches—both good and bad ones.

Chaparro saw to it that the informer was given refreshments, and then he sent for MacNally who had bivouacked his men in their usual place outside the bandits' encamp-

164

ment. Chaparro, who knew the news of Fletcher's activities would make the *americano* gallop out to begin a series of wild chases, chuckled to himself as the American soldiers once again blew bugles and bustled around before going in pursuit of the swordsman again.

Chaparro turned his attention to Gomez. "I am glad to see that you still wear your *Rurale* uniform. I am not about to gallop aimlessly all over the desert looking for that bastard Fletcher. I have a plan to bring him to me, and you—along with your uniform—will be playing an active role in it."

Gomez wiped the chili sauce from his chin and grinned. "*A su servicio, Jefe*—at your service, Chief."

Chapter Nineteen

The survivors looked up at the *Rurales* with dull, listless eyes. The ranch that had once been home to a wealthy rancher and a large crew of *vaqueros*—Mexican cowboys—was little more than tumbled down adobe and charred lumber. Fresh graves with brand new crosses gave evidence of two dozen recent deaths.

"How long ago did this happen?" Moreno asked one leathery-faced *vaquero*.

The man doffed his *sombrero* respectfully. "Three days, *Señor Capitán*, it is only through the grace of the good *Dios* and our fierce determination to resist that we were able to drive the *diablos* off."

"*Ustedes fueron muy valientes*," Moreno complimented him. "Although many men died, you saved your women from any outrages."

"Yes," the man said sadly. "Yet they weep for the dead. But we killed many of the *indios* too. They were very careless, these Apaches. They made reckless charges like they thought our bullets would not kill them."

Tanaka Tom looked with respect on the graves of the fallen. Glorious deaths such as these would guarantee a better existence in the next life. Surely these brave Mexicans would be reborn samurai. He dismounted and walked over to offer a few moments of respectful meditation when he suddenly stopped and studied the ground. Then he rushed back to where Moreno and the *vaquero* talked. "There are many tracks here in the yard," Tanaka Tom said.

"We are a ranch, *Señor*" the Mexican said. "Naturally there is always much riding back and forth here."

"But there are many tracks of horses shod in a peculiar fashion. . . ."

"Ah! The *gringo* soldiers," the man interrupted. "Yes, they passed through here. Too late to help us. But isn't it strange that the *Americanos* were down here?"

"How long ago were they visiting?" Tom asked.

"They left about *dos horas* two hours—ago, *Señor*," the *vaquero* said. "Pardon me, is that a sword you are wearing?"

"Yes," Tom answered impatiently. "Which way did they go?"

"Out the opposite side you rode in on. They went west," the man said. "Please, *Señor*, why do you wear a sword?"

Tom ignored the question as he and the *Rurales* mounted up. At a shouted order from Moreno the detachment galloped from the ranchyard and found the tracks left by the American cavalrymen. Osote, who was doing the tracking for the group, looked up happily. "They are traveling slowly, Cuchillo Largo."

"Then before this day is done we can deliver your message to this interloper," Moreno said.

"If he doesn't shoot us down first," Tanaka Tom warned him. "Terrance MacNally is as fanatical in his way as El Mesias is in his."

The *rurale* stood on his saddle and waved the white flag back and forth slowly. Over in the distance, through the haze that danced above the desert floor, the American troops seemed a smudge on the horizon. But a sharp-eyed Osote caught the movement. "They are waving a flag too, Cuchillo Largo."

"Fine," Tanaka Tom said. "Let's go out and see how we can deal with Captain MacNally."

A three-man delegation from each group rode forward toward a central meeting place. Tanaka Tom, Moreno and Osote reined up several yards short of MacNally, Lieutenant Martin, and another officer.

MacNally grinned. "You're taking a hell of a chance, Fletcher. You're wanted by the American authorities and I have every right to arrest you."

"I'm not wanted—you are," Tom said. He dismounted and walked up to Lieutenant Martin. "These are from Colonel Breckenridge."

"Breckenridge!" MacNally exclaimed. "Phony papers, no doubt. Read them, Mister Martin."

"Yes, Sir." The young officer quickly scanned the orders and then turned to his commander. "We are ordered to return immediately to American soil without taking part in any more activities against Apaches, Sir."

"What the hell are you talking about?" MacNally demanded. He looked at the papers, then crumbled them up and threw them to the ground. "False! They're false, goddammit!"

"Oh, no, Sir!" Martin said artlessly. "I recognize the colonel's signature, the adjutant's and—"

"Forgeries!" MacNally cried. "And I'm not fooled by them."

"Sir . . ." Martin was uncertain as to how to handle the situation. He looked to the other officer, an older captain named Brandon. Then he dismounted and retrieved the orders, handing them to him.

Brandon looked at the signatures. "They're genuine, Terry. We've got to obey and return quickly across the border."

"No, by God! I've got this bastard Fletcher, and I'm not letting him get away again!" MacNally fumbled at his holster and drew the Colt .45 pointing it directly at Tanaka Tom. "Now I've got you, you slimy bastard!"

"No, Sir!" Martin yelled. He instinctively reached out and hit his commander's hand. One wild shot zoomed off into the desert sky before the pistol fell to the ground.

"By God, Martin, I'll—" Before MacNally could say more, Tom had stepped forward and literally flipped him from the saddle with one deft move. The officer sat up in the dust, his face contorted with rage. "Goddamn you to hell, Fletcher!" he hissed. He leaped to his feet and rushed forward but quickly found himself rolling in the dirt again.

Tanaka Tom's face remained passive. "You will also note in those orders that I am to be left alone and unmolested."

By then, Martin and Brandon had dismounted. Both rushed forward and grabbed MacNally. "Forget it, Terry," Brandon said. "Let's get back to Fort Bozie."

"We have no choice, Sir," Martin said.

By then MacNally's mind had returned to a rational state. Though still angry, he realized his predicament. His gaze drilled into Tanaka Tom Fletcher's eyes. "One day I'll get you, Fletcher! I may have to track you down like an animal or trap you like an escaped convict, but I'm going to nail your hide to some wall. You can count on it."

Tanaka Tom said nothing as the officer was led away by his peers. Francisco Moreno laid a hand on the samurai's shoulder. "You must constantly be careful, *amigo*," the *Rurale* captain said. "You will always have an enemy in the world as long as that man stalks the earth."

* * *

The Apache warrior absent-mindedly rubbed his empty belly. He had been so long without food that the sensations and feelings of hunger were dulled to being scarcely noticeable. He only knew he felt weak, a little dizzy and in dire need of sustenance. A movement at the bottom of the trail he was guarding caught his eye and he tried to shake his dizziness and clear his vision to see who or what it was that approached.

The man wore a *Rurale* uniform. The alarm that had crept into the Apache's being diminished. He could remember *Capitán* Moreno and his men who were friends of Cuchillo Largo. He waited for the man to draw abreast of his guard post before he stepped forward.

"*Saludos*," Oscar Gomez said, smiling. Acting under Chaparro's instructions, he had ridden up to visit the Apaches in their Duro Mountain stronghold. "I am looking for the headman."

"That is Brujito, our medicine man," the Apache said. "He is in the village somewhere. Ask anybody."

"*Gracias*," Gomez said. "I have good news for all of you." He rode on up the trail and entered the village. He nodded politely to a group of hungry squaws and inquired for the location of Brujito. Again he mentioned good news for everybody as he let his horse amble slowly across the camp to the spot where the shaman's crude wickiup stood.

Brujito watched the policeman approach with growing interest. He had the Apache's instinctive distrust of Mexicans, but he realized the men of the *Rurales* had been working with Tanaka Tom Long Knife in this long struggle of survival. "*¿Qué quieres?*" he inquired of Gomez.

"My *capitán* and your friend Long Knife have sent me to fetch the people here and take them to a meeting place," Gomez lied with an oily smile. "We have defeated the *bandidos* in a big battle. And the *gringo* soldiers too. You can return to the United States now. Everything is fixed up. There is food as well." Gomez reached back into his saddlebags and produced a fresh hunk of venison. "See? We *Rurales* have shot many deer. There will be a dance and feast when you get there."

To Brujito's primitive mind, the entire situation was wrapped up. In his simple, savage outlook the defeat of a group of enemies completely removed any problems. Complicated logic was beyond his comprehension and Gomez's lies seemed truthful enough. The Apache grinned widely, then rushed out to the center of the village, waving his arms. "Everybody listen! Cuchillo Largo has sent for us! All our enemies are dead."

Paloma ran over from her wickiup and grabbed his arm. "Are you sure of this, Brujito?"

"Yes! Yes! See the *Rurale*? Your man Cuchillo Largo has sent him to lead us to where they wait. There will be a feast and even a dance. Everybody hurry!"

Even as the sounds of joy began sounding throughout the Duro Mountain camp, down below Chaparro's men were already moving into ambush positions.

Chapter Twenty

El Mesias peered through the vegetation, then looked back at Lagarto with an approving smile. "You did well," the youthful leader said. "As usual your tracking proved accurate and fast."

"It was not too difficult," Lagarto said modestly. "After Alcito spotted the pony soldiers arguing with the Mexican and Cuchillo Largo yesterday, it was easy to find them."

"I cannot figure why they didn't fight," El Mesias said. "Nor why the soldiers turned north and left the others in peace. But right now I am happy to have the interloper Fletcher and those cursed *Rurales* in our grasp."

Slightly below them Tanaka Tom, Osote and Francisco Moreno led the detachment of *Rurales* across the vast emptiness as they still sought the very men who were now looking down on them from the scrubby heights that dominated the area.

El Mesias trembled in his excitement until he could contain himself no longer. "Thunder Eagles!" he shrieked. "Attack!" He waved his amulet stick toward the *Rurales* in frantic flourishes as his warriors kicked their ponies' flanks and galloped up and over the ridge.

Tanaka Tom turned in his saddle at the shouts to see the first line of Apache warriors sweeping down at them.

Francisco Moreno, ever the soldier, shouted his first battle orders to form his men up for the coming fight.

Several *Rurales* were pitched from their saddles by Apache bullets and their riderless horses hindered the attempts to form up and meet the fanatical attackers now closing with them.

El Mesias' warriors bowled into the column as the combatants formed a whirling, screaming mass. Carbines were useless in the tightly packed battle area, so knives, tomahawks, clubs, pistols and Tanaka Tom's *katana* were brought into the fight.

Tom, feeling hindered on horseback, slid from his saddle and lashed out quickly at the nearest target. The brave screamed as the sword blade bit deep into his side, then reeled before falling to the ground, staring in horror at the massive wound through which his life now flowed. A second warrior dove from his horse and caught the samurai's shoulders, knocking him to the ground.

Tanaka Tom rolled with the momentum of the fall and was back on his feet in an instant. He pivoted, bringing the *katana* into a horizontal stroke that split his assailant's chest open. A graceful reverse of the same slice sent the head spinning off the Apache's shoulders to bounce wide-eyed, mouth agape into the dust.

Another follower of El Mesias leaped screaming from his pony and raced across the space between himself and Tanaka Tom holding out his lance for a fatal jab. Tanaka Tom, almost serenely, chopped off the lance head, then quickly shortened the weapon's staff with lightning fast slices until it lay on the ground—with its owner's severed hands still grasping it. The warrior stood in shock, but a quick and merciful stab up under the rib cage caught his heart and put an end to the numb misery.

As the Six-gun Samurai's *katana* sang death songs for three more attackers, Francisco Moreno finally got his men into position and was able to order the first disciplined volley of the battle.

The crashing thunder spilled several Apaches to the ground as other *rurales,* now able to disengage from the hand-to-hand fracas, joined their comrades.

171

El Mesias' warriors hesitated, then attempted an attack into the *rurale* formation where Tanaka Tom and Osote now added their own weapons to the massed gunfire that Francisco Moreno directed so skillfully. The rain of bullets that slammed into the Thunder Eagles braves dropped several into crimson heaps.

Two more volleys took their toll before the Apaches, unused to a determined and disciplined enemy, pulled back. Another volley convinced them to keep moving and they ran to the safety of the ridge over which they had just attacked a scant twenty minutes before.

They were losing the battle—and knew it. Wide-eyed and confused, they looked around for El Mesias and the guidance he would provide them. He was nowhere to be seen. Soon the sounds of fighting died out altogether until an eerie silence dominated the scene.

"Look to me!" The voice sounded from above and all, Apache and *rurale* alike, turned to gaze up at the tallest bluff some sixty feet above them. El Mesias, resplendent in his Thunder Eagle costume, stood on the edge with his arms outspread. Again he shouted, "Look to me!"

The fighters on both sides gazed in wonderment at the magnificent sight of the young man standing there. The eagle feathers on his sleeves looked almost like real wings from that distance.

"I am not El Mesias!" The voice trembled but was firm. "I have become Thunder Eagle! *Thunder Eagle! THUNDER EAGLE!* And I shall fly down and strike my enemies dead!"

Suddenly El Mesias dove off the cliff in a graceful arc and plummeted straight to the base into a shattered heap of broken bones and punished flesh.

After several moments of silence, Osote suddenly rushed forward between the two fighting forces. He looked first at El Mesias' corpse then over to where Lagarto and the other warriors stood.

"He was only a man! Not a god!" Osote shouted. "Nor a friend of Thunder Eagle. And now look at him. He lies dead because he is punished for blaspheming our great war deity. And you will die too if you do not renounce his teachings and return to your people. Do so now! Do not wait or Cuchillo Largo and I, with our Mexican friends, will destroy you once and for all.''

Tanaka Tom joined his friend. ''Your women and children wait for you in the Duro Mountains. We have been promised that the pony soldiers will not bother us if we return peacefully to the Ancha Mesa. When we tell them of El Mesias' death, they will be satisfied.''

Lagarto suddenly appeared on the ridge line, staring down at Tanaka Tom Long Knife. He raised his tomahawk high above his head and walked down toward the samurai in a steady, measured gait. Tom tensed as the young warrior drew closer. He eased the *katana* in its scabbard for a quick draw, his hand resting on the hilt.

Lagarto walked up to a point some ten feet from Tom. He stared at him stonily for several long seconds, then his face twitched and quivered as tears flowed from his eyes. He dropped the tomahawk to the ground and knelt down with bowed head. ''You were my friend, Cuchillo Largo, and I deserted you for a false leader. I am ashamed and seek punishment. Do with me as you will, Cuchillo Largo.''

Tanaka Tom, who had felt great anger both at the youth's impetuous following of El Mesias as well as the personal betrayal he committed, fought his anger. His first reaction was to send the *katana* blade singing through the boy's neck, but he realized he was dealing with a person whose background and attitudes had been formed in a near stone-age environment. Lagarto's values and ideals were on a basic primitive level, but he had the personal and physical bravery to be faithful to whatever he believed in. And to admit it aloud and in public when he had been wrong. Very few so-called civilized men could truthfully claim such admirable qualities.

''Come with me, Lagarto,'' Tanaka Tom Long Knife said. ''Be my friend again and become a leader of your people. They need a man like you who will stand up for them and who is not afraid to die to defend them.''

173

Lagarto, overcome by emotion, nodded his understanding. Other warriors, some looking sheepish, began drifting down until all stood around Osote and Tanaka Tom, waiting to be told what to do.

"We will give El Mesias to *Capitán* Moreno to take to his leaders," Tanaka Tom said. "And all of us will go to the Duros to fetch our people. The *rurales* have promised to go with us to help us fight bandits if necessary."

There was a general stirring among the two groups as the wounded were tended to and others went off to gather up horses who had wandered away during the fight. Finally, after an hour, they formed up and rode out toward the mountains where they thought the rest of the Ancha Mesa people awaited them.

Fear and anger danced across the faces of the Apache warriors. They had ridden to the Duro Mountains in happy anticipation of once again being with their women instead of having to rely on rapine for sexual pleasure. Their loincloths had been strained by the hardened burdens that pushed against them until they reached the trail that led up to the stronghold.

There they had found two dead Apache boys—both scalped—and signs of a brief struggle. Any warrior there could tell that a group of mostly women and children had been surrounded by horses shod in the Mexican manner. Scuffs in the dirt gave evidence of brief struggles before the hapless captives were driven off.

Osote and several other warriors galloped down the trail from their reconnaissance on the mountain. The Apache leader's face was grim as he reined up in front of Tanaka Tom Long Knife.

"Cuchillo Largo!" he exclaimed. "There is no one left in the camp. Somehow they were all lured down here. What terrible magic brought this about?"

"There was no magic involved here," Tanaka Tom said. "Rather deceit and treachery."

Capitán Francisco Moreno nodded his agreement and spoke the one word that was in all their minds. "Chaparro!"

"Yes," Tanaka Tom said. "And our confrontation with that devil is at hand now."

"We will need the blessings of the sacred Virgin of Guadalupe," Moreno said. "We are going to have one hell of a fight, *amigo*. Chaparro is no fanatical crazy man like El Mesias. He is calm, cool, and logical. And the leader of the toughest bandit gang in Mexico."

"You already have El Mesias to your credit," Tanaka Tom said. "That will make you hero enough in the eyes of the Mexican people."

"Ah, *Sí!*" Moreno said. "But to add Chaparro to my list of conquests would make my heroism superlative, no?"

Tanaka Tom grinned at his Mexican friend. "I think there is more bravery here than ego, Francisco."

"Of course," Moreno said with a grand gesture. "But even a magnificent fellow like me can have a bit of modesty."

Osote's patience was at an end. "Let us ride to do battle *now!*"

"Yes," Tanaka Tom said. "To glory—or death."

"*La gloria o la muerte*," Moreno said, repeating the phrase in Spanish.

*　*　*

Chaparro stood with his most trusted aides as they looked down on the Apache prisoners herded into the center of their camp. The few warriors who had been separated from the women and children stood in a sullen group off to one side.

"They are not too healthy," one of the *bandidos* complained.

"They are starving," another added in displeasure. "Look at them. Their ribs are showing."

Chaparro laughed. "But the scalps will still fetch fancy prices in Nogales, *muchachos*." He signaled to his men who stood with ready carbines behind the male prisoners. "*¡Ya! ¡Matanlos!*"

A sudden, unexpected explosion of simultaneous gunfire ripped across the area. The warriors were slammed into

175

jerky little dances of death before they collapsed to the ground under the impact of the slugs.

A *bandido* rushed forward with his scalping knife drawn. He worked rapidly until at last he stood up with a bloody trophy held high in the air.

Chaparro laughed loudly. "You are slow, Manuel!"

"It is not my fault, *Jefe*," the bandit shouted back. "The *cabron* was still alive and twitching. It is more difficult that way."

"Then don't waste time, *muchachos*," Chaparro said. "Get to work on the others." He glanced over to where Paloma held her infant son Pumito tightly in her arms. They stood with the other women and children. "Then the *real* fun begins," he added with boisterous laughter.

Chapter Twenty-One

The bandit walked up to the tearful, frightened Apache woman. She clung to her baby, fearful defiance in her eyes. Suddenly the man ripped the child from her grasp and tossed it as high into the air as possible. The little infant wailed as he fell to the ground with a thud. The little bundle whimpered only a moment before the high heel of the *bandido's* foot slammed into his head. The mother screamed and tried to rush to her dead offspring, but others of Chaparro's men grabbed her and dragged her away for sport.

Other children were grabbed and the women, their motherly instinct to protect their children driving them to insanity, attacked the bandits. The men struck them with clubs, whips and carbine butts as others began cutting the Apache children's throats to dispatch them more quickly. Several of the young—mostly pre-teens—had scampered into the group of mothers. These children screamed in terror as the *bandidos* managed to chase them all down and dispatch them with repeated blows to the head with pistol butts.

The only two among the group to be spared were Paloma and Pumito. Chaparro had seen to it that they were pulled away from the turmoil and brought to him.

Chaparro glared at the woman, his eyes filled with hatred. "I am going to kill that heathen *bastardo* you carry in front of Fletcher's eyes, you Apache *perra!*" he hissed. "Then I am going to make him watch while I fuck you until your eyes bug out. There won't be an opening in your body that will not overflow with my sperm. Not a millimeter of your flesh will be unviolated."

Paloma, her usually strong fortitude shaken but still hanging on, stared back at him, her flashing eyes concealing the fear she felt. "My man will cut your flaccid penis from your body, *mexicano,* and feed it to the coyotes."

"*¡Basta!*" Chaparro screamed and struck her across the face. Paloma fell to the ground, then rolled over to put her body between Pumito and the enraged bandit chief. Chaparro delivered a vicious kick to her buttocks that sent her sprawling again. "I will make coin purses from your breasts, *puta india!*"

The bandit's own women and children watched the sport from a respectful distance. Although most of the women felt a slight amount of jealousy, watching their men enjoy the Indian women, they were glad these usually crude lovers would be spent and weary by the time night fell. Their children grinned and winked at each other at the men's antics, although several boys in their early teens were clearly becoming excited at the sexual activity before them. When they began eyeing the females of their peers, the mothers wisely ushered the girls away.

Chaparro turned Paloma over to his personal bodyguards for safekeeping, then walked back to where the naked Apache women, legs spread and held by bandits, were still enduring the sexual assaults. Teeth marks across their breasts showed the hateful lust that was being applied to them.

"Keep the women alive if you wish," Chaparro said to his men. "We will not leave for Nogales until tomorrow. You can play with them and enjoy them until dawn. Then they must be scalped."

The *bandidos* cheered the good news and turned back to their games. Laughter burst out as one of the attackers suddenly screamed in pain. He had forced his manhood into the mouth of a teenage Apache girl who had bitten halfway through the member in her rage. The bandit, his bleeding penis spreading crimson down his trousers, kicked the girl to death amid the protests of his comrades.

The orgy created so much noise and attracted such a great amount of attention in the bandit camp that no one, including the distracted guards, noticed the silently moving force of *rurales* and Apaches easing into carbine range. Finally the young daughter of a *bandido* who had reached the terminus of her attention span for the spectacle, let her eyes wander into the distance. She caught sight of the unexpected visitors and tugged at her mother's skirt. *"Mira, Mamacita, ya vienen mas hombres para jugar,"* she said.

Her mother looked down at the child. "What other men are coming to play?" she asked.

"Ellos. Them," the girl said pointing to where Tanaka Tom, Osote, and Francisco Moreno led their combined forces toward them.

The woman, puzzled at first, soon made out the unmistakable uniforms of the Mexican lawmen. She shrieked an alarm, but it went unheeded. She raced down toward the scene of rapine, waving her arms. Her efforts cost her a *rurale* bullet flush in the face and her cranium exploded like a watermelon in the hot sun.

The sound of that shot, plus the others that now sent slugs slamming into the bandits, finally alerted Chaparro and his men. The rapists struggled with their trousers leaving their weeping victims as they sought the guns they had left in a convenient pile. One Apache woman took advantage of her tormentor's distraction to bring a foot up into his scrotum in a vicious kick. His scream was cut off by the bullet that sent his jawbone whirling through the air. He grabbed at his mutilated face and staggered in agony until two more rounds hit him, pitching the bandit to the dirt.

Tanaka Tom, Colt .45 in one hand and *katana* in the other, felt the battle lust swell up as he led the charge through the prostrate Apache women who now screamed encouragement to their men and the *rurales*.

Both sides locked together in a whirling, dust-flying battle that brought them face-to-face. It was one of those close-in affairs, where a man stood as much of a chance of dying from strangulation as from a bullet. But the advantage was clearly to the attackers. The surprise, combined with the shock of their assault and the hatred of the Apaches, was clearly going to be the telling point in the battle.

The *bandidos* began slowly falling back at first, leaving dead and wounded strewn before their disorganized ranks. These unlucky ones had their skulls split open by tomahawks and carbine butts as Tanaka Tom and his men pushed on relentlessly in the screaming crush of combat.

A small gap developed between the two forces as the bandits' haphazard formation began folding in. This left their leader Chaparro exposed to view in time for Tanaka Tom to leap forward and confront him. The two stood tensed for the first move of the impromptu duel. The rest of the fighting died off until the battlers of both sides stood watching their leaders.

Chaparro, sneering and disdainful, took off his gunbelt and tossed it away. Then he reached behind and produced an American Bowie knife. "Let us have this out Mexican style, Fletcher," he snarled. "If you have the balls for it."

Tanaka Tom answered the challenge by quickly disarming himself, keeping only his *tanto*, the dagger used by the samurai. He suddenly wished he'd had time to don his armor for an occasion he considered near sacred. He held the dagger out and announced loudly to the crowd that watched:

"I am Tanaka Tom, adopted son of Tanaka Nobunara and an officer of the Fujika *Rentai*. This man has challenged my honor by offering me personal combat. I order that no one interfere in this fight—no matter how it progresses."

Chaparro grinned wickedly and shouted to his own men. "You will do the same, you miserable *cabrónes*. This fight is a private one."

Both sides cheered as the duelists began cautiously circling each other.

Chapter Twenty-Two

Tanaka Tom stepped back from two quick feints by Chaparro and countered with a slashing attack that made no contact but at least kept the Mexican at a distance.

Chaparro lunged and withdrew in one quick motion that caused the samurai to extend his arm slightly more than was safe. The bandit chief, his reflexes tuned and sharp, delivered a cut that went through Tom's jacket and into his arm. The wound was not deep nor did it hit any arteries. Chaparro laughed. "*Primer sangre*. First blood."

"It's the last that counts," Tanaka Tom said. He jabbed as Chaparro jumped back from the attack, made a horizontal stroke to continue the assault and finally a slash that missed the upper body but bit into the *bandido's* thigh. "*Segundo sangre*," Tom said in Spanish.

"If you had been more to the left I would be a *señorita*," Chaparro said in macabre humor. "Maybe that's what I'll do to you, Fletcher. Cut off your *huevos* and carve a *culo* in there for me to fuck. I bet you'd be good in bed that way, no?''

"I know nothing of such things," Tanaka Tom said. "The idea of slipping between the blankets with a man never comes into my mind."

Chaparro's Latin *machismo* attitude was rattled by this implication that he had homosexual tendencies. He responded recklessly with a quick, yelling rush that earned him a badly slashed cheek from a much calmer Tanaka Tom. The Six-gun Samurai smiled. *"Trecera sangre."*

Chaparro realized his mistake and took time to calm down as he circled warily around his skillful opponent. He suddenly stopped moving and stood deathly still for several long moments as his eyes locked with Tanaka Tom's. Then the Mexican quickly exploded into a violent but carefully controlled attack that left Tanaka Tom with another cut in his knife arm and one in the shoulder.

"Cuarta y quinta sangre," Chaparro said.

Tanaka Tom's shoulder wound was deep and bled badly. At least it wasn't in his left shoulder. The southpaw fighter, the right arm hanging limp, leaped forward to attack, then shuddered, his knees almost buckling. He drew back on unsteady feet.

Chaparro sensed his advantage. *"Arriba!"* he shouted in triumph. This time his attack was meant to be a killing one. The space between himself and Tanaka Tom closed in one swift millisecond.

But the Six-gun Samurai wasn't there.

Chaparro spun and felt his knife hand caught up in the samurai's left hand, the grip sure and steady, showing that the weakness displayed moments before had been false. He desperately tried to push his weapon toward Tom. The samurai, wanting exactly that, took advantage of the motion to pull with it. Chaparro found himself propelled along a path he didn't wish to follow. Then Tanaka Tom pulled the bandit's arm up in another distinct move. The Mexican's feet kept going

181

as he crashed to the ground, his knife flying from his grasp.

Tanaka Tom Long Knife's last words were quiet and calm, yet rang with a chilling finality: *"Ultima sangre— last blood!"*

The *tanto* sliced deep into Chaparro's throat and the blood spouted like a fountain at first, then eased into a steady flow. Death was almost instantaneous.

Tanaka Tom sat his Morgan stallion, Paloma with Pumito on her back safe and secure in the papoose carrier behind him, grasping his waist with her head happily pressed into his broad back.

The carnage of the former bandit camp had already attracted the vultures who circled overhead in squawking impatience as they waited for the last of the Apaches and *rurales* to leave.

Francisco Moreno rode up and saluted the samurai. "This is where we part company, eh, *compañero*?"

"It would seem so," Tanaka Tom said. He extended his hand. "It is an honor to have fought at your side."

"And one for me too," Moreno said. He pointed to the two pack horses his personal orderly was tending in the distance. One held El Mesías' corpse, the other that of Chaparro. The *rurale* captain grinned widely. "You know, *amigo*, within twenty-four hours after I ride into Nogales and deliver those two dead *diablos*, I will be a general."

"Congratulations," Tom said. "I hope to see you again."

"Igualmente," Moreno said. *"Adiós,* Thomas Fletcher, you are one of a kind."

Tom only smiled as the officer led his detachment away. Then he took one more look at the area that used to be dominated by Chaparro.

The final act of battle had been the overwhelming, near spontaneous charge of the combined Apache-*Rurale* force that left mutilated, burned and dismembered bodies scattered through the old camp. The bandit's women, ravished by *rurale* and Apache alike, bore only single

182

or double wounds that had brought about their demise. Their children had been dispatched with blows to the head.

But the *bandidos* themselves had obviously died worse. Those not lucky enough to have been killed outright in battle had given up the ghost slowly and in agony over Apache fires. Nothing Tanaka Tom Fletcher could do or say had put a stop to the atrocious vengeance. Old scores were settled between Apache and *bandido* as well as *rurale* and *bandido*. The only survivor of Chaparro's men was Oscar Gomez, the deserter from Moreno's detachment. He was in irons and was to be taken back to Nogales to the inevitable firing squad.

Paloma nudged her man. "The battle is over, *hombre mío*. It is time to return to the Ancha Mesa."

Tanaka Tom nodded, then gently urged his horse forward after the column of Apaches that even then moved north toward the American border. A sudden pounding of hooves caught his attention as Lagarto rode up. The youth smiled widely. "Another great victory, eh, Cuchillo Largo?"

"*Seguro*," Tom agreed.

"When we get back to the Ancha Mesa, let's go hunting," Lagarto said.

"Only if you promise not to make me part of the game this time," Tanaka Tom said, grinning.

Lagarto, his face somber for just an instant, caught the joke. He responded with loud laughter as they headed out onto the Sonoran desert.

Epilogue

Tanaka Tom Fletcher picked up the brush and dipped it in the ink. He thought for several moments before touching it to the rice paper that lay in front of him.

Honored Father and Mother,
   I humbly report that I have been through yet another battle and have undeservedly emerged victorious through some fluke of the gods. Although this did not involve my quest to avenge my family against the evil Edward Hollister, I feel I may have helped some friends. This little affair deserves no mention and is unworthy of your attention except to say that the antics of a mad-man caused terrible tragedy for innocent women and children.
   I leave now for the state of Idaho where I hope to find a certain Dudley Sanders. My friend General Mat-thew Tomlinson has informed me of the evil being done by this former member of the 251st Ohio Volunteers. He is but another step on this long journey.
   All my best wishes to honorable parents from a most unworthy son.

Tanaka Tom Noburana

Tom rolled up the paper, then stood up and walked to where his Morgan stallion and pack mule waited. He placed the message in his saddlebags for future mailing as Paloma gathered the writing materials and put them away in their place in the pack.

Then she joined him. "When will you return to us, *hombre mío?*"

"When I am in need of rest and comfort," Tanaka Tom said.

Osote, who stood in front of the crowd of Apaches

gathered around the wickiup, smiled. "We hope you are able to recuperate with more tranquility next time, Cuchillo Largo."

Tom nodded as he swung up in the saddle. "Any time you need me, send for me."

Paloma looked up shyly. "When you come back next year you will have another son. Once again your seed grows in my belly."

The crowd laughed and cheered the news. Osote grinned broadly. "You will end up making me an uncle many times over, Cuchillo Largo."

Tom only waved, then pulled up on the reins and started back for the trail that led down to the flatlands.

Once there, his mind occupied by the deadly task ahead of him, he gave no more thought to the Ancha Mesa as he turned north toward Idaho.